ECHOES OF SILENCE

DI SALLY PARKER #15

M A COMLEY

Copyright © 2024 by M A Comley

All rights reserved.

No part of this book may be reproduced in any form or by any electronic or mechanical means, including information storage and retrieval systems, without written permission from the author, except for the use of brief quotations in a book review.

❦ Created with Vellum

To my mother, gone but never forgotten. Miss you every second of every day, Mum.

ACKNOWLEDGMENTS

Special thanks as always go to @studioenp for their superb cover design expertise.

My heartfelt thanks go to my wonderful editor Emmy, my proofreaders Joseph and Barbara for spotting all the lingering nits.

A special shoutout to all my wonderful ARC Group, who help to keep me sane.

PROLOGUE

Fifty years ago

"I SAID, get on your knees, boy. I've warned you about disobeying me, and here you are, doing it all over again."

Tommy Wise glanced over his shoulder at the other boys in the class. Trembling, they were all too aware of what was about to happen to him.

He put a hand on the school desk beside him and hesitantly lowered himself onto one knee. Tommy screamed when the thin cane smacked the back of his hand.

Mr Styles laughed raucously as Tommy's discomfort came to the fore.

"Please, sir. No more," Tommy mumbled, his gaze glued to Mr Styles' highly polished black lace-up shoes. He dared to raise his head to gauge the level of anger Mr Styles was displaying and soon wished he hadn't when the cane lashed against his right shoulder. He knew better than to cry out. His punishment would be so much worse if he did.

"Don't tell me what to do, Wise, or you'll have more consequences to deal with, you hear me?"

Tommy knelt and nodded. This time, he kept his focus on the floor beneath him.

"I'm glad we understand each other. I'm curious as to why you're the sole person who hasn't handed in their homework. I want the truth, boy."

Tommy swallowed and whispered, "I was ill, sir."

"That's news to me. Did you see the nurse?"

"No, I went to bed early."

"That's no excuse. I've warned everyone in this class what would happen if their homework wasn't handed in on time. Sometimes I'm ill, but I still show up for work. You need to man up, boy. We're here to teach you to cope with life after you leave us. Do you think it'll be all right to take to your bed when you're ill in the future? Skip work for the day?"

"No, sir. I'm sorry, sir. Please forgive me."

"Ah, if only that were possible. You know my rules, three mistakes and it's off to the headmaster's office."

"But... but..."

"No buts. Hold your hand out."

Tommy held his hand out and squeezed his eyes tightly shut. He tried hard not to react when the cane smacked his palm, not just once, but three times in quick succession.

"I'm sorry, sir, it won't happen again."

"The trouble is, Wise, I don't believe you. Get up and go to the corner of the room. I want you to pay attention to what's being said here today, because after the class has ended, I'll expect you to recite everything."

Tommy raised his head, and his gaze met his tormentor's. "Yes, sir, I'll try."

The cane made contact with his left shoulder this time. "You'll do more than try. Now, get off your knees, move to the corner of the room, and then get back down on your knees again. I'm sure the other boys will have a word with you later about you holding up the class, as now the lesson will be eating into their break time."

"I'm sorry, sir," Tommy muttered and scrambled to his feet and changed his position. His only mistake was to sneak a look behind him when he got down on his knees again.

Styles thundered towards him, his face beet red with anger. "Are you taking the piss, boy?"

"No, sir." Tommy was unsure what he'd done this time to upset his teacher.

"Turn around, moron. Actually, no, don't bother. Get to your feet." Styles grabbed Tommy by the ear and assisted him to his feet. He faced the other boys. "Read the first chapter of *Treasure Island*, boys. I'll test you on it when I return. Wise and I are going to take a trip to the headmaster's office. I will not put up with insubordination in this classroom. Let this be a warning to the rest of you."

Still holding Tommy's ear in a vice-like grip, Styles marched the eight-year-old out of the classroom.

Tommy was never seen again.

1

Present day. Wednesday, January 3rd

DI Sally Parker forced herself out of bed and into her en suite bathroom, leaving Simon still snoring gently. They'd had a week off together, and it had been magical. Thankfully, the weather had been kind to them and allowed them to take Dex on various walks around Norfolk. She had been working flat out at the station for months and hadn't had a holiday since May, which wasn't entirely her fault. Simon's business had been non-stop, too, in that time. Spending time together had been just what they'd both needed to recharge their discharged batteries.

Lorne, her more than proficient partner, had insisted that Sally should take time off. Sally had expected Lorne to be on the phone at least every other day, but she hadn't. She should have known that her partner and the team would be capable of wrapping up the last case they'd solved.

Her partner had dropped by occasionally during the week. She only lived next door, so it wasn't like she'd had to go out of her way to see Sally. Lorne had kept things brief, not wishing to burden her during her break. Sally appreciated her partner's willingness to keep her at arm's length. But now the time had come to show her face at the office again.

She showered and dried her hair in the spare bedroom, rather than disturb her husband. When she returned to their bedroom, he was missing from the bed. The door to the en suite was open, so she knew he wasn't in there.

A few minutes later, Simon appeared with a tray full of breakfast goodies as she was tucking her cream blouse into her black skirt.

"What are you doing? I would have fixed myself some breakfast and brought you up a coffee before I left."

He placed the tray on the end of the bed and turned to kiss her. He wrapped his arms around her, and the kiss deepened, taking Sally's breath away.

"Wow, what was that in aid of?" she asked, amused.

"Just showing you how much you mean to me, in case there was any doubt. Come on, your toast will get cold."

"There are never any doubts in my mind, Simon. Thank you for doing this for me."

They sat on the bed close to each other and tucked into their breakfast. It didn't take long for Dex to appear at their feet.

"Never one to miss out on an opportunity, hey, boy?" Sally sniggered. They never fed him while they ate but always saved him the last piece of toast on their plates.

Sally gave Dex the corner of the toast and drank the rest of her coffee, then peeked at her watch. "I'd better get a move on, or I'll never hear the end of it from Lorne. What's on the agenda for you and Tony today?"

"There's the first auction of the year taking place. Tony suggested we should go, thinking it might be quiet at this time of year."

Sally cocked an eyebrow. "Seriously? I would have said the opposite, all the fathers trying to escape their squabbling tribes."

"That was my thought. We'll see how it goes. If it turns out to be too busy, we'll come away and put our heads together. We've got one property due to be finished next week. We're on the lookout for another project to ensure the men keep working."

"Poor timing, lack of judgement, which was it?"

"Cheeky cow, neither. The trouble is, our guys are so efficient that they're keeping us on our toes. Take a week off and it can upset the applecart."

Sally slipped on her suit jacket. "Ah, here it comes. This is where I get the blame, isn't it?"

He laughed. "Hardly. We were both in dire need of a break."

She bent to kiss him. "I won't argue with you on that score. I need to clean my teeth and get on the road." With that, her phone jingled. "Damn, that'll probably be Lorne pestering me."

Simon reached for her phone. "Yep. She's asking if you're running late."

"Bugger. Can you message her and tell her I'll be with her in five minutes?"

He unlocked her phone, sent the text and received a thumbs-up emoji back from Lorne.

Sally came out of the bathroom and stood in front of Simon. He placed his hands on either side of her waist, and she bent to kiss him. "Have a good day and thank you again for breakfast. Call me later, if you get the chance. I'm bound to be snowed under with paperwork. I'll probably need the distraction today."

"I'll see how the day goes. If I can, I will. Hope you don't have to deal with too much crap when you get there."

"Famous last words. See you tonight. Have a good one."

She left the house and drove the short distance to pick Lorne up, who was waiting on the pavement.

"Sorry, we had breakfast in bed this morning, well, sort of," Sally said.

Lorne held her hand up in front of her. "Er... too much information. I bet you're glad to be going in to work today."

"Not really, but them's the breaks. How was your weekend?"

"Busy shovelling dog poo, as always."

"Damn, you should have given me a shout. I would have lent you a hand."

Lorne shot her a look. "Really?"

Sally grinned. "Er... no. I was joking. Why on earth would I choose to shovel shit at the weekend when I do enough of that during the week at work?"

"Because you had the week off and missed out last week."

"Ah, yes. You've got me by the short and curlies there."

"The question is, do you feel rested?"

"Absolutely. I hope you didn't have too much to contend with last week."

"No, it was a breeze."

THEY ARRIVED AT THE STATION, and Lorne made them both a

coffee. They were still ten minutes early and the rest of the team hadn't arrived yet.

Sally poked her head around the office door and groaned. "What the heck?"

"Hey, I did my best. There's a pile on the right that I wasn't sure what to do with. I could have bugged you about it while you were off, but I didn't think you would appreciate that."

"You're a wise old bird," Sally ribbed. She took the mug from Lorne's hand and said, "If I'm not out in an hour, you have my permission to come and rescue me."

Lorne laughed. Sally closed the door and stopped to admire the view, or what there was of it. The mist hovered low over the open fields surrounding the station, making visibility non-existent this morning. She settled into her chair and took a sip from her coffee, then tackled the post in her in-tray.

After dividing it into piles of urgency, she spotted a handwritten envelope that piqued her interest. Ever cautious, she slipped on a pair of latex gloves and opened it.

DEAR DI SALLY PARKER,

IT HAS TAKEN me many years to reach out and find someone who would be prepared to listen and act upon the information I'm willing to share with you. I write this letter with a heavy heart and a soul burdened by the weight of memories long suppressed by others. Fifty years have passed since the horrors I endured as a child at what was supposed to be a sanctuary, a boys' school nestled in the heart of our community. But behind the grand exte-

rior and the façade of respectability lay a darkness that still haunts my every moment.

I BELIEVE the staff at the school should be held accountable. They knew what was happening. Ashamedly, they turned a blind eye to the torture, to the secrets and lies that festered within those walls. They knew of the concealed dead bodies, the rooms where sinister things happened to innocent children like me. They knew, and yet they have remained silent, complicit in the unspeakable crimes that stained the very foundation of that property.

FOR YEARS, I have carried the scars, both physical and mental. To this day, the nightmares continue to torment me. But I cannot remain silent any longer. It is time to speak out, to seek justice for those who suffered at the hands of monsters masquerading as caretakers.

WILL YOU HELP ME, DI Sally Parker? Will you be the voice that finally breaks the deafening silence that has shrouded the truth for far too long? I'm at my wit's end. It has taken me years of torment to find the strength to put pen to paper, to reach out to the police once more, even though there were people who let us down when we needed them the most.

I BEG OF YOU, do not let the sins of the past remain buried in the shadows. Uncover the truth, reveal the horrors that were inflicted upon us and hold accountable those who sank to such depraved depths. I'm pleading with you to help me find closure and bring to justice those who are still alive.

Yours sincerely,

A concerned member of the community

Sally's eyes instantly filled up with tears, and she reread the note a couple more times, not believing what she'd read the first time.

A knock on the door interrupted her on her final read-through.

Lorne opened the door and stepped in. "I've come to... Sally, what's wrong?" Her partner rushed forward.

Sally gulped and shook her head.

Lorne plucked a tissue from the box on the desk and handed it to Sally. "You're worrying me. What's wrong, love?"

Sally removed another glove from the small drawer beside her and handed it to Lorne. "Put this on."

"What? Why?"

"You'll soon see. Just do it."

Lorne snapped the glove in place and took the letter from Sally.

"Read it." She watched the emotions come and go on her partner's face.

Once Lorne had read the contents of the letter, her gaze met Sally's, and she said, "What the actual fuck?"

Sally pulled a tissue from the box and repaid the favour. Lorne wiped her eyes and blew out a breath. "Hard to believe, isn't it?"

"And then some. Do you know where this place is?"

"No idea, not yet, but I'm determined to find out. There's no way I will allow this to go unpunished."

Lorne shook her head. "Just hold fire, take a step back. We don't know how factual the letter is. Why sign it anonymously?"

"God, wouldn't you?"

Lorne tilted her head. "Is that a serious question?"

"Of course it is."

"Honestly, Sally, we're going to need to tread carefully here."

"I refuse to sit back and do nothing, Lorne. I'm surprised you would even consider doing that."

"You're getting this all wrong. All I'm saying is that you should take what's written in that letter as…"

"What, with a pinch of salt? You read it. This person has been sitting on this information for fifty years, apparently going through emotional trauma every single day."

Lorne closed her eyes and let out a deep sigh. "I know. I'm with you one hundred percent, but I'm throwing in a word of caution, that's all."

"I appreciate that. Never has a letter evoked such images for me. I despise anything to do with abuse, especially towards innocent children, and that's from someone who hasn't got kids, or never wanted them."

Lorne fell silent. It took Sally a few moments to work out what was behind her partner's silence.

"Shit! I've put my foot in it, haven't I?"

Lorne smiled and shook her head. "Don't be silly. I'm not denying it didn't cause some flashbacks for me, but it goes with the territory. There are some shitty fuckers walking the streets. We're both aware of that."

"But fifty years ago?"

"I suppose abuse of one form or another has been prevalent in our society for centuries."

"I don't know how you coped, you know, when Charlie was kidnapped by the Unicorn. I would have been a quivering wreck, inconsolable had it been my child. Instead, you dug deep and refused to give up on her."

"I had an excellent team around me, and at least two good things came from the ordeal."

Sally narrowed her eyes as she thought. "I can think of one good thing: Charlie overcoming the adversity to become a copper and getting on with her life. What's the other one?"

"You're funny. It was during that time I met Tony, even though in the beginning, I despised him."

"Gosh, er, dare I say that you also had a fling with Jacques Arnaud around then, as well?"

Lorne stared out of the window and, again, Sally could have kicked herself for opening her mouth without engaging her brain first.

"Jesus, I've done it again, haven't I? Will you ever forgive me?"

Lorne glanced her way and wiped her eyes. "Don't be silly. It's been a while since I've thought about Jacques and what might have been if that bastard, the Unicorn, hadn't killed him. I suppose I'll always feel guilty for involving him. Turning to him for a shoulder to cry on when my husband, Tom, didn't want to know and continued to treat me like shit."

"That period of your life must have been mind-blowing."

"Yeah, you're not wrong. But life goes on, and everyone has their crosses to bear. I can categorically say that was the most depressing time I've ever had to contend with. However, it's the positives we all need to cling to in this life."

Sally sighed. "Ain't that the truth? Determination and willpower help, too." She reflected on the significant mountains she'd climbed over the years, during her disastrous, abusive marriage to Darryl. Who was now serving time behind bars.

"God, we've definitely both been through the mill, haven't we?"

"They say what doesn't kill us makes us stronger."

"That's true for us, which is why I have no intention of ignoring this letter or the information it contains. It could be the biggest cold case investigation we've ever encountered."

"That's a scary thought. Where should we start?"

"We'll run it past the team first. Most of them are local, maybe something will resonate with one of them. Did Charlie have a good time over Christmas?"

Lorne smiled. "She did. Tony and I tried working on her to get her to see sense about moving up here and leaving London, but she's adamant that she wants to stay down there."

"The best thing is not to force the issue with her, Lorne. All you can do is show her how chilled you've become since moving up here, and that goes for Tony, too."

"She knows. I can't help but worry about her, especially with what keeps surfacing through the news about the Met."

Sally picked up a pen and twiddled it between her fingers. "I suppose there's one way of looking at it. It might be a good time to be down there, now that the spotlight is trained on them."

"Yeah, I suppose you're right. It's what lies beneath which is causing me concern."

"I can understand that. After what you went through

during your couple of spells down there. You didn't have it easy, did you?"

"That's an understatement. That's why I'm worried so much about Charlie. I fear she's not as strong as she wants us to believe."

"Because of a certain period in her life?"

"Exactly."

"I think you're probably more conscious of that incident now. She seems okay to me, and I've spoken to her a lot over the years. I can't say I've ever had any doubts about her mental state."

"In other words, I'm being overprotective because I'm her mother."

Sally grinned. "That's a mother's job, surely? What about Tom? Is he still on the scene?"

"Last I heard, he was hitting the bottle, and his marriage was in tatters. I try not to be the one to raise that subject. I believe Charlie is at the end of her tether with him. He showed up at the station a few months ago and made a fool of her. I'm not sure she's forgiven him for that little stunt yet. His behaviour appalled me, but then when I sat back and thought about it, I realised that's the type of thing I had to contend with daily when I was married to the prat."

"So glad you escaped and that you've found true happiness with Tony now. He's a good man. Simon is always singing his praises."

Lorne smiled. "They make a great team. Just like us."

"Yep, right, that's enough of the small talk now. We'd better get cracking on this."

"Do you think you should run it past DCI Green, first?"

Sally chewed her lip and stared down at the note. "Not wishing to deliberately keep him out of the loop, but I'd like to see what the team comes up with first, before I get him involved."

"Makes sense to me."

"I'll be out in a second. I want to run off several copies, then I can send the original over to the lab for them to deal with."

"One of the lads will drop it off for you if you ask them nicely."

Sally grinned. "Here's hoping."

Lorne left the office, and Sally sat there for the next few minutes, rereading the letter. The same emotions she'd experienced before stirred within. It was obvious there was no way she'd be able to ignore what the author had written. Some of her predecessors might have if the letter had landed on their desks, but not her.

She wiped away another stray tear and ran several copies off on the printer behind her. Then she tucked the original back into the envelope and popped it in an evidence bag. After that, Sally joined the rest of the team in the outer office.

"I haven't mentioned it," Lorne said when Sally glanced her way.

"Thanks. Okay, team, a new investigation has suddenly appeared on my desk this morning in the form of a letter." Sally distributed a copy to each member of her team and watched their responses.

"What?" DC Jordan Reid asked. "Is this for real, boss?"

Sally hitched up a shoulder. "That's for us to find out. Does anyone have any idea where this place might be?"

"I think I might," Joanna Tryst said. She turned to her computer and punched the keyboard, then swivelled the screen around to face the rest of the team. "I seem to recall hearing rumours about this place, Oakridge Hall, when I was a youngster."

Sally approached Joanna and bent down to study the enormous building. "What sort of rumours?"

Joanna shrugged. "As far as I can remember, it was the worst kind."

"That place has been lying empty for decades. Has anyone else got any information on it?" The others shook their heads. "Okay, let's see what we can dig up about it and we'll go from there."

SEVERAL HOURS LATER, with everyone doing their best, a sinister image began to emerge concerning the former manor house.

"How could such a beautiful place turn into such a den of iniquity?" Lorne asked.

"More to the point, why wasn't anything done about it? All the rumours have been rife since then, but there was nothing at the time, not from what I can see." Sally shook her head in disbelief. "Moreover, I can't believe that I've lived here my whole life and didn't even know about this place."

"I'm with you there, boss," Jordan said.

"I've not heard of the place," Lorne said. She viewed the image of the property on her screen. "It's beautiful, or should I say, it must have been, in its time. It has extensive grounds, set in fifteen acres. It's got a woodland off to the right. Looking at the aerial shots, it's set well back from the road. If the total area is overgrown, I'm not surprised you haven't heard about it. What a shocking waste to let it fall into disrepair like that. Nothing in this life makes sense when that type of thing is allowed to happen."

"Let's not judge a book by its cover. We shouldn't do that, given what we've just read and what Joanna has told us. Who owned it?"

"The council owns it now. The last owner died, and no members of his family are left. Which meant it went back to the government. They passed it on to the council to deal with," Joanna informed her. "Maybe that's why it's been left to perish."

"Appalling situation. That place could have been renovated over the years and given refuge to many homeless people," Sally said.

"That's your property developer's brain kicking in," Lorne replied.

Sally sniggered. "I suppose so. I hate to think of places of distinction going to waste, though."

"During the war, it used to be a makeshift hospital," DC Stuart McBain, the last member of their team, said.

"Interesting, and then it became a school in the late sixties, after being left empty for decades," Sally said, as she read the history of the building on the screen. "Has anyone found any articles in the newspapers about the place?"

"Strangely, not yet," Lorne replied.

"That is surprising. Especially if there were rumours about it. Can you remember when these rumours surfaced, Joanna? Or can you tell us who told you?"

"I'm trying to cast my mind back. Mum and Dad used to hold a lot of dinner parties when I was a child. I think I overheard something I shouldn't have heard during one of those. When I asked Mum about it the following day, at first, she seemed shocked by the question, then she told me I must have misheard it. Afterwards, she got annoyed with me. I'm presuming because she realised I could hear what was being said at one of their parties."

"Okay, let's keep digging, folks. I think I should run this past DCI Green before we proceed." She swept past Lorne's desk. "Wish me luck."

"You've got this. He'd be foolish to ignore the letter. Just tell him the person who wrote it might end up taking it to the press if we don't deal with it first."

Sally laughed. "Christ, that's sure to put the wind up him." She walked along the corridor to Green's office. Lyn Porter was at the coffee machine when she entered the room. "I must have smelt it on the go."

"You're welcome to join us for one if you have the time."

"Brilliant, you know I never say no. Is he available?"

"He's making a quick personal call. He informed me he wouldn't be too long."

Sally lowered her voice and asked, "How's he bearing up? He told me his wife had walked out on him a few months back."

"The divorce is looming, and suddenly, she's decided that she wants the house. He's in a tizzy about it."

"I think I would be, too. Maybe I should call back and see him another time."

With that, the office door opened, and DCI Green emerged. "Hello, Inspector. Have you come to see me?"

"Umm... I wanted a quick chat with you, sir. It doesn't matter if you're busy. I can come back another time."

"No, I had a personal issue to sort out. Come through. Put your order in with Lyn first." He turned around and went back into his office.

"White with one sugar?" Lyn asked.

Sally rubbed the secretary's arm. "You're a treasure, thanks, Lyn." Out of courtesy, she knocked on the door before she entered Green's office.

"Come in, Inspector. There's no need to knock, not if I've

already told you to come in," he said once she'd opened the door.

"Sorry, sir."

He pointed at the letter in her hand. "I'm surmising that your visit has something to do with that?"

"It has, sir." She sat opposite him and passed a copy of the letter over the desk.

He read it, glancing up at her a few times throughout. "What the fuck? Are you taking this seriously?"

Lyn entered the room and deposited their coffees on the desk.

Sally waited for the door to close again and replied, "I think we should, sir."

"Fifty years ago. I know you're a cold case team, but even that's stretching the limits a bit, isn't it?"

"Is it, sir? My team and I have been doing some digging on the place, and I have to say I've been disappointed with the results we've found."

"That should be enough to tell you to leave well alone then, shouldn't it?"

Confused, Sally frowned. "Sorry, you're going to need to explain your train of thought to me, sir."

He shuffled the papers on his desk as he thought. "I'm just saying, how often has something like this, I mean receiving an anonymous letter, backfired on the investigating officer?"

"I can't answer that because, to my knowledge, I've never received a letter in the post before, not of this nature. I think it would be foolish of us to ignore it."

He picked up his cup, blew on his drink and said, "Then go ahead, but be careful."

"I'm always careful. I just feel it's important for us to at least go there and have a nose around."

"If you can get in."

"We won't know unless we try."

"Do you have any other investigations on the go right now?"

"No, we're wrapping up the details on the two cases we've recently solved. I've instructed the team to do that before we jump in and begin this one."

He glanced out of the window.

Sally could tell he was distracted and dared to ask, "Is everything okay, sir?"

"Yes and no. As you know, I'm not one for bringing my problems to work."

"I know. But a problem shared and all that."

He faced her and shook his head. "Not this time, Inspector. What's done is done, and there's no going back."

"Are you talking about the separation from your wife?"

"Didn't I tell you? We're getting divorced. Out of the blue, she's told me she wants the house. The trouble is, it was my parents' home, and I don't think she has a right to it."

"Can you buy her out? Or pay her off would probably be a better way of putting it."

"I can, but I've got this niggling doubt about that. Why should I? The property was my family home and... It's getting messy. I shouldn't burden you with my problems. Let me know how you get on with the investigation. If I were you, I wouldn't spend too much time on it."

"Do I have your permission to get SOCO involved? There might be a necessity to take down a few internal walls."

"Yikes, I never thought about that. We'd better do things properly and get a search warrant ASAP."

"I'd already considered that. I'll give the lab a call. Speak to the pathologist, get her primed and ready."

"Let's hope she isn't needed."

Sally sipped at her drink. "I hope that's the case, too. Umm... if you ever need to chat, I'm always available," she said tentatively.

His gaze dropped to his cup. "Why do we put ourselves through this?"

"Through what? Marriage?"

"Yes. I thought I had a solid marriage until a year ago. How wrong I was. Still, there's no turning the clock back or dwelling on what might have been. We're past the point of no return now. Things have been said on both sides, that shouldn't have been."

"So sorry to hear that. I was going to ask if marriage counselling might be the answer."

"No, we tried a couple of sessions. She ended up walking out on them. I didn't bother suggesting it again. Nope, I have to face the fact that this time next month, I'm going to be a single man. Not what I was expecting to deal with at forty, I can tell you."

"My heart goes out to you, sir. You'll get through it."

He smiled and said, "The voice of experience talking?"

Sally smiled and nodded. "Believe me, after bailing out of my miserable, abusive marriage, I never dreamt I'd be this happy."

"You had the advantage of knowing Simon professionally before you started dating. What chance do I have of meeting anyone stuck in the office all day, every day?"

"I know. I could lend a hand there."

He frowned and asked, "What do you mean? You have enough on your plate as it is."

"We could hold a barbecue back at the house and invite all our single friends to it."

He gasped. "Shit! I couldn't think of anything worse to attend, but thanks for the offer."

Embarrassed, Sally took a large gulp of coffee and ended up choking. It took her a while to regain her composure.

He rushed to fetch her a glass of water from the outer office and handed it to her. "Here, take this."

"I'm so sorry. I don't know what came over me."

"Hush now. Drink."

She took a couple of sips, and the cold water eased the rawness in her throat. "Bloody hell. That caught me out. Please forgive me, sir."

"Nothing to forgive. It could happen to anyone. How are you now?"

"Apart from feeling foolish, in more ways than one?"

He laughed. "You don't have to feel that way. I appreciate what you were trying to do with your suggestion. It's not for me, though."

"It was worth a try. I'd better go and splash some cold water on my face."

"Let me know how you get on with the investigation. It could prove to be an intriguing one."

"And an emotional one, no doubt. I will. And, sir, you know where I am if you ever need a shoulder to cry on."

"Thank you, I'll remember that, Inspector. I'll be fine once I get my head around a few things. I have an excellent solicitor on my side. He seems to think it's a no-go for her, but you know how notorious judges are for coming down on the woman's side."

"I hope not, for your sake." She left her cup and saucer on the desk and exited the room.

"Everything all right?" Lyn asked, concern written all over her face. "I hear you had a choking fit in there."

"I'm fine. I must have gulped down a lot of air at the same time as my coffee. It's all good now. I got a bit flustered because it happened in front of the boss."

"Embarrassment count at its maximum, eh?"

"You could say that. Nevertheless, the coffee was wonderful."

"Even if it nearly killed you."

They both laughed. Sally stopped off at the ladies' toilet on the way back to the office. She dabbed cold water on her reddened cheeks and watched the colour fade back to near normal, thankful that there were now no more lasting effects of her traumatic event.

She returned to the incident room and, on her way through to her office, she asked Lorne to put in a request to obtain a search warrant. Then she rang Pauline, hoping to catch her before she started for the day.

"Hello, Inspector. To what do I owe the pleasure?"

"Have you got time to talk?"

"Yes, you caught me typing up a few PM reports. What can I do for you?"

Sally explained the situation to her and asked what her opinion was.

"Blimey, okay, that sounds intriguing. Have you checked out the background information of the place concerned?"

"We're delving deeper now. What we know to date is that Oakridge Hall was a makeshift hospital during the war. After that, it was empty for a couple of decades before it became a boys' school."

"Interesting. And you say you're getting a warrant now?"

"That's right. There's no telling how long that is likely to take to come through. I wanted to give you the heads up first. Perhaps you can prepare your team, just in case we need to get in there at a moment's notice."

"Don't worry, we'll be there. I can feel the excitement stirring within me already. Damn, I shouldn't have said that, should I?"

"You're forgiven. I get where you're coming from. I'll be in touch soon."

"We'll be ready and waiting for the go-ahead. Enjoy the rest of your day."

"I'll try. I'm going to get back to it. The more we can find out about this place, the better prepared we'll be later, once we're able to get in there."

"Good luck."

Sally ended the call and sifted through the couple of letters she'd set aside while attending to the urgent anonymous one.

Lorne knocked on the door ten minutes later with another cup of coffee. "Thought you might need this."

"Thanks. I'll have it coming out of my ears soon."

"Oops, want me to take it away again? Did the chief give you one?"

Sally grinned. "A coffee? Yes."

Lorne flopped into the chair opposite her. "How did he take it?"

"He said to surge ahead but be cautious; that was before I had my coughing fit and made a fool of myself."

"Oh heck, what a nightmare. I hope he was kind to you."

"He was. I had to stop off at the loo to splash water on my cheeks."

"Poor you. What was his take on the letter?"

"I watched his reaction as he read it. He appeared shocked by its contents. You'd have to be cold-hearted not to be affected by it. I wish it wasn't anonymous. If anything, that's what is making me doubt its authenticity. Until we find something of value there, I'm going to have the same doubts running through my mind."

"I suppose that's why we need to remain open-minded about this, for now."

Sally nodded. "What would you do if you were in charge?"

"The same thing you're doing right now. Have you prewarned the lab?"

"Yes, I've just finished talking with Pauline."

"And what was her take on it?"

"Pretty much the same as ours. She's excited about the prospect of unearthing God knows what there."

"Excited? Should we be worried about that?" Lorne chuckled. "She's a strange one."

"It's better than her constantly having a go at me, so I'll take it. I'm eager to get on with things. I wonder how long the warrant will take to come through."

"I'd say at least a couple of days. In the meantime, we need to get cracking on finding out what we can about the place."

Sally scratched her head. "I have to say, I haven't heard anything on the grapevine over the years. I'll ask Simon tonight and see if he knows anything."

"He might surprise you. There would be no point in asking Tony, what with him being a Londoner, like me."

"Maybe the team could ask their relatives. The ones who are from this area." Sally chewed on the inside of her mouth. "I think we're going to need all the help we can get."

"It might be worth putting out an appeal in the future."

"Not yet, though. I wouldn't want to end up with egg on my face. That could happen if I call one too soon. Do you fancy dropping by there on the way home this evening?"

Lorne rubbed her hands together and beamed. "Yeah, I'm up for it."

"Good, okay, that's settled then. My head is spinning with different images. What's the betting I don't sleep tonight?"

"No, don't say that. Christ, if you're reacting like this already, what are you going to be like if we discover any bodies at the site?"

"I know. I must put it out of my mind, for now."

Lorne rose from her chair. "I'll leave you to get on with your paperwork and I'll help with the research."

"You're a star. Thanks, Lorne. We'll sneak off early tonight, at around five-thirty, okay?"

Lorne rubbed her hands together again, like an excited teenager. "Sounds like a good idea to me. I'll be ready and waiting."

SALLY SAID farewell to the rest of the team and, as scheduled, she and Lorne left the station and drove out to Oakridge Hall. "Christ, look at the state of this place."

Lorne withdrew her phone from her pocket and showed her an old black-and-white photo of the building taken in the forties.

"It's soul-destroying to see it. The comparison is stark."

The gates to the property had long been stolen, although the stone pillars and arch remained. Sally put the car into gear and gently rolled forward, shaking her head as she drove. "Unbelievable. Can you imagine the impact our other halves would have on this place?"

"I can imagine how many zeros it would take to do up a place like this. It would bankrupt all of us."

"You're not wrong."

Sally drove down the long, winding driveway, past a lake overflowing with weeds at its edges, and came to a stop outside the main house. The front door was still intact, which surprised them both.

Sally and Lorne exited the car and approached the front door.

"Worth a try, right?" Sally grinned cheekily. She twisted the doorknob, but it refused to budge. "Bummer. I know I was chancing my arm. Geez, this place is enormous, far bigger than I thought it would be from that photo."

"Based on the information we've gathered so far, it has a total of fifty-six rooms."

"Blimey, fancy that. Damn, what if we have to search every room?"

"I think that's a given if that letter is to be believed."

"Shit, it's just dawned on me the mammoth task that lies ahead of us."

"It would be better if we didn't think about it, otherwise, there's a chance you might regret taking the case on. In my opinion, it's going to take a bigger team than we first expected."

"I'm thinking the same." Sally turned to survey the extensive grounds. "Besides the lake, there are a few outbuildings to take into consideration, as well. Shit! It's going to be a never-ending task."

"Yep, that's true."

"Come on, let's go home and try to put this place out of our minds until the search warrant gets approved."

Lorne laughed. "As if that's going to happen. I mean, you not thinking about this place."

"You know me so well, or think you do."

Lorne gave her one of her looks and rubbed the back of her hand a few times.

Sally growled and said, "Get in."

DEEP IN THOUGHT, she dropped Lorne off twenty minutes later and continued home. Simon had just pulled up and was at the rear of his Range Rover, seeing to Dex.

Sally parked and walked across the gravel to greet them. "Hello, you two. Have you had a good day?"

"Let's say we achieved a lot and leave it at that. What about you?" Simon frowned and studied her features.

"It was okay. I'll tell you about it inside. What are we going to have for dinner?"

"Why don't you take Dex for a walk? It looks like you need it, and I'll worry about dinner. I've got something in mind, but it's a surprise."

"You're so good to me. Okay, we won't be too long."

"Take as long as you need. It seems like you're carrying the weight of the world on your shoulders, love."

"Sort of. Thanks for understanding, Simon. Come on, Munchkin, let's go for a stroll down by the river."

Dex barked, leapt out of the back of the car and barked some more as he twisted first one way and then the other.

"Okay, settle down," Sally warned. "Or we can forget about our walk and have a run around the garden instead."

Dex instantly calmed down, allowing her to attach the leash. She pecked Simon on the cheek, and then she and Dex set off on their evening walk. No matter what kind of day she had, this was the part she enjoyed the most. Even if she felt dead on her feet after an exhausting day, time with her pup was all she needed to unwind, to rid herself of the day's pressures and disappointments. She sensed she was going to be snowed under with stress shortly, if the investigation went ahead.

Once they were by the river at what she assumed was a safe spot, Sally removed the leash and permitted Dex to jump into the river. Even though it was only four degrees, Dex was adamant about submerging himself in the water and rescuing the bigger stones from the riverbed.

He returned the stones to dry land and dropped them at Sally's feet.

"You're nuts. Here, fetch." She threw the stone back in the water, not once, but another dozen times or more, until she thought enough was enough and called an end to the game. "Come on, Dex, out of the water now."

Dex glanced up and wagged his tail from the middle of the river, knowing that she couldn't get in there and drag him out. She was prepared for every eventuality and undid the zip of the bumbag she'd slipped on before setting off.

Withdrawing a treat, she held it out and said, "Come and get it."

Dex hesitated, thought about diving his head under to retrieve another stone, but then thought better of it and splashed out of the water to sit in front of her. She patted him on the head and broke the treat in two. "You're a good lad. Eat it slowly."

Dex did the opposite and immediately gulped down the chew and wagged his tail for the second part. Sally gave it to him and attached the leash to his harness without him realising it, foiling his attempt to defy her and jump back into the river again.

They walked home, sometimes guided by the torch on her phone in the areas where the streetlights had been removed. "Damn council, they never consider the pedestrians in an area, only the drivers." She upped her pace, and they arrived home five minutes later. "We're home," she shouted.

Simon failed to answer, obviously engrossed in getting their dinner ready, being the perfectionist he was in the kitchen. She dried Dex with the towel they kept in the cupboard by the front door and then went through to the kitchen to check on Simon.

He glanced up as he tasted the sauce he was preparing in the frying pan and winked at her. "Simply divine. You've got time to change if you want to."

"Great. I'll be five minutes." She shot upstairs and removed her work suit, which she placed over the comfy chair in the corner, and then slipped on her velour suit, or her *old faithful* as she liked to call it. After running a comb through her hair, she returned to the kitchen to find Simon plating up their meal.

"Take a seat."

She did as he'd instructed. The table had been laid and a glass of wine was waiting for her. She sipped her drink until he joined her.

Simon put the plate in front of her. "Enjoy."

He had prepared steak smothered in a creamy peppercorn sauce, one of her favourites, together with baby potatoes, broccoli and carrots.

She marvelled at the exquisite meal he'd conjured up for them in under half an hour. "This is impressive. If I were still living on my own, it would have been a jacket potato, beans and cheese night for me. It's incredible how fast you can knock up a meal of this calibre. What would I do without you?"

"Either starve or bang on weight, having to rely on takeaways all the time. Dig in, I'm starving."

"Me, too. Did you find a house at auction today?"

"We did. It's huge. After chatting with the builder, we think we're going to develop it into six flats."

"Will the Planning Department go for that?"

"They're going to have to accept conversions like this as the norm soon, given the rate at which the market is moving and with so many people unable to afford larger properties."

"Good luck getting it through. Where is it?"

"Hethersett, so it is still within thirty minutes of home, which is what we try to aim for when selecting our properties."

"That's great." She fell quiet and tucked into her steak. "This is the best steak we've had. Is that down to the way you've cooked it?"

He smiled. "I'd like to take credit for it, but Wayne, the butcher, told me he'd sourced a new supplier and gave me the steaks, knowing I would give him genuine feedback."

"Really? Well, it's top marks from me."

"I'll pass that on to Wayne the next time I visit him. I must admit, it's the best I've tasted in a long time. Not that the meat before was substandard, but this is exceptionally good." He took another mouthful, chewed it, and then asked, "And how was your day? I could see the stress seeped into your pores when you came home. That's why I suggested you go for a walk with Dex."

"That's what I love about you, your ability to know when something isn't right and your willingness to let me mull things over before asking me what's going on."

"Thanks. Are you ready to talk about it now?"

"Can we leave it until after our meal? I've been upset about it all day and the last thing I want is to be put off my dinner while spilling the details."

"Hey, that's fine by me. It's your call, love. Are you sure you're okay?"

"I'm fine. Tell me more about the property."

"It's an old manor house in desperate need of love and

attention. It bugs the hell out of me the way people give up on their homes. Once the neglect goes too far, this is the result."

Sally nodded but still didn't say anything about Oakridge Hall.

Simon eyed her cautiously. "Are you listening to me? I get the impression that while your body is here, your mind is elsewhere."

"Sorry, you might be right." She finished her meal, pushed her plate to one side and took another couple of sips of her wine. "Why don't I clear up in here and then we'll have a chat in the lounge over another glass of wine?"

"We'll tidy up together. You wash and I'll wipe. How's that? Many hands make light work and all that."

"Agreed."

It was almost seven by the time they'd cleared up the kitchen and fed Dex. They took their wine glasses and the rest of the bottle through to the lounge.

Sally sat next to her husband and clasped his hand. "What do you know about Oakridge Hall?"

His head jutted forward, and his eyes widened. "Er... why do you ask?"

"Because that's our new investigation."

He frowned and took another sip from his glass before he answered, "Investigation into what? That place has been closed for years."

"So you do know it? How?"

"My father went to school there for a few years."

Sally leaned forward, gobsmacked by the revelation. "What? You're not winding me up, are you?"

"No, why would I do that?"

Sally ran a hand around her face. "I don't know. It's just that we've been searching for the background of the manor house today, and while we loosely know what it has been over the years, there's little else out there for us to sink our teeth into."

"But why would you want to?"

"Sorry, I should have started at the beginning, instead of what happened halfway through my day. First thing this morning, I was carrying out my least favourite chore when I came across a handwritten letter. Wait... I'll be right back." She ran upstairs, collected a copy of the letter she had tucked away in her jacket pocket and returned to the lounge. "Here, have a read of this and tell me what you think." She passed him the letter and eagerly watched on to see his reaction.

Now and again, he glanced up at her with tears in his eyes. Eventually, he returned the letter to her and shook his head. "My God. I can't believe what I've just read. No wonder you appeared stressed when you got home. Do you know which school they're referring to?"

"My team has conducted extensive research all day, and we're positive it's Oakridge Hall."

His mouth gaped open for a second or two, and then he whispered, "I can't believe it. I wonder if Dad had any issues there when he was a boy."

Sally's heart raced. "Do you think I could have a word with your dad about this?"

Simon shook his head. "I'd rather you kept him out of it, given his poor health. You know what Mum said at the weekend."

Sally's shoulders slumped, and her sudden enthusiasm waned. "I'm sorry, it was wrong of me to ask. Can you recall what he used to tell you about his school days?"

"God, now you're asking. Let me think about it."

"There's no rush. Lorne and I dropped by there on our

way home this evening. It's huge. It's going to be a daunting task when we finally get the go-ahead to search it."

"I've never really seen it. As far as I can remember, Dad was quite open about his experience there. I think his parents had to go abroad to Africa for a year and enrolled him in the school. I think his stay was extended when my grandfather was taken ill with malaria and couldn't travel."

"So, he spent longer than expected at the school. That's interesting. Did he say if he was happy there or can't you recall him telling you that?"

"No, it's a bit fuzzy. I believe we only discussed it twice. Each time we spoke about it, I got the impression he was being reticent about the facts."

"So, you didn't want to push it, is that it?"

"Correct."

Sally scrolled through her phone to the link Lorne had sent her and showed her husband the image of the property.

"Geez, you've got a task and a half on your hands there. What state is it in now?"

"We haven't gained access to the inside yet. I'd be inclined to label it as severely run-down, without going so far as to classify it as derelict."

"It will not be easy. I do recall Dad telling me he used to get lost frequently whilst staying there."

"I'm not surprised. We've learnt that it has fifty-six rooms."

"Shit! That's going to take you months to search."

"I know. It wasn't until I saw the place in the flesh that I realised the extent of what lies ahead of us. Daunting isn't a word I like to use during an investigation; however, it fits the bill for this one."

"If there's anything I can do to help, all you have to do is ask, love."

"I appreciate that, hon. We're desperate to know more facts about what went on there when it was up and running as a school."

"I'm sure people will come forward if you put out an appeal for help."

"Lorne and I discussed this earlier. I'm reluctant to call on the public yet. Not until the search begins and we find something worthy of further investigation."

He tilted his head, his brow furrowed with half a dozen wrinkles. "Maybe you should reconsider that?"

"I can't. I think this might turn out to be a case of going with my gut feelings, especially to begin with."

He nodded. "Hmm... there's something to be said about gut instincts in your line of business. I remember what that used to be like. Do you fancy a top-up?"

Sally emptied her glass and offered it up for more.

He filled it halfway and then topped up his glass to the same level. "Pushing the negatives aside, here's to a successful investigation. I hope it doesn't prove to be too traumatic for you."

"Umm... there's one thing you can do for me if you wouldn't mind?" she asked falteringly.

"Name it. You know me, I don't mind helping when I can, eager to keep my hand in."

"Would you mind asking your mum if we could have a chat with your father about his experience at the school? When he's well enough, of course."

"I can try, but you know how protective she is when it comes to Dad's health."

"I get that. It would be better if we had an unbiased opinion from someone I can trust, such as your father. I get the sense that when word gets out, people might stick their spoke in and offer a web of lies. You know what it's like during an investigation of this magnitude."

"Sadly true. There are dubious members of society who will do their utmost to prevent the police from getting to the truth."

"Exactly."

Then Sally changed the topic of conversation, having discussed everything they had learnt thus far about Oakridge Hall. "When will you hear whether the conversion can go ahead?"

He grinned and winked at her. "I'll have a word with the architect. He's got a friend who works in the Planning Department who usually pushes things through for us."

"What it's like to have friends in high places, eh? I wish that happened to me occasionally. It would definitely make my life easier now and again."

"Aww... poor you. Here, I'll give you a cuddle instead."

They cuddled and drank their wine until Simon went quiet. Sally, who had her head rested on his chest, looked up to find that he'd drifted off to sleep. Thinking it was too early to hit the sack, she switched on the TV and flicked through the channels, turning it off again a few minutes later, disappointed at what was on offer on terrestrial TV. Simon stirred beside her.

"Come on, sleepyhead, why don't we chuck the towel in and have an early night? You go up and I'll see to Dex."

He smiled sleepily and yawned. "It's been a tiring couple of weeks. I'm not used to having all this time off over Christmas and the New Year."

"I know what you mean. Do you want to take our drinks upstairs?"

"It would be a shame to waste them."

2

Over the next few days, life was fraught for Sally and her team. They dug in places they had never had to dig before during an investigation to get to the truth, and still, it evaded them. Sally had thought at one about contacting her ex-commanding officer, who had spent forty years on the force and retired a couple of years after he'd promoted her to inspector. The last she'd heard was that Bill Salford was living out the rest of his days in a care home, having lost his wife to cancer five years before.

After she'd run the suggestion past Lorne, they decided she should take a step back and leave visiting Bill until they had something concrete to go on.

The longer they were left up in the air about obtaining the search warrant, the more the team's frustration grew. Sally was wound up like a coiled spring, especially after Joanna informed her that the warrant had once again been delayed. As she entered her office that morning, Sally vented her anger by kicking out at the spare chair.

Lorne followed her into the office. "Hey, these things

happen. You're going to need to stop getting wound up about it."

Sally sank into her chair and growled. "Ugh... I just want to get in there and see for myself what it's like. It's not too much to ask, is it?"

Lorne returned the spare chair to its rightful position and sat in it. She smiled and shook her head. "I know. Believe me when I say this, every member of this team feels the same way. We've been going over the same ground relentlessly for the past three days, and it's already feeling like we're banging our heads against a brick wall."

"I know. Sorry, I didn't mean to sound so selfish. It was wrong of me to vent my anger. I should be able to control my emotions, but the sleepless nights are racking up this week. All because of my desperation to get in there. It's the not knowing that is tearing me apart."

"No, it's probably your active imagination that's doing the damage. You need to learn to relax. We all know there's nothing more we can do except wait right now."

"I suppose what worries me is the possibility of another investigation coming our way in the meantime. If we ever get into Oakridge Hall, we're going to be stretched to the limits as it is, without having to deal with the added distraction of another new case."

"I get where you're coming from. I truly do. My advice would be to stop worrying about things that have yet to happen. Look at the state you're getting yourself into. It's just not worth it."

Sally closed her eyes and, after a moment's contemplation, she nodded and opened them again. "Why are you always right?"

"Years of practice," Lorne laughed. "No, seriously, if I were in your shoes, I would sit back and give myself a good talking-to. What's the point in getting worked up when certain things are out of your control?"

"Okay, I'm chilled enough to tackle this shit now." Sally spread her hand over the piles of envelopes sitting on her desk. "I've already checked, and there are no further handwritten ones."

"Well, that's a blessing. Do you want me to check with the council about getting a key for Oakridge?"

"Yes, if you would, one less job for me to do. I hope the author of the mysterious letter isn't thinking badly of me. Maybe he thinks I've binned it and I'm not taking the contents seriously. I'm presuming it's a *he*, given that the hall used to be a boys' school."

"I figured that out for myself." Lorne grinned and rose from her chair. "I'll leave you to it. You should regard today's onerous task as a much-needed distraction."

"I will, thanks. And if you fancy bringing me another coffee in half an hour, I'd appreciate it."

"Consider it done."

Lorne left her office, and Sally started up her computer to check her emails. There was one in particular that caught her eye. She opened it and read the message out loud.

Dear Sally Parker,

I must say, I expected more from you. I didn't think you would let me down like this, not in a month of Sundays. Still, I don't know why I should be surprised, not really. The police have never been any good in Norfolk.

Yours,
Concerned member of the public

Sally responded to the email. Told the person that she had put the wheels in motion, but it was taking time to get a search warrant for the premises. Then she added:

Please come forward *and talk to me in person. I promise to keep your identity a secret, for now at least. Your original letter hinted at grave events occurring at Oakridge Hall, but we could do with more details to conduct our inquiry. Therefore, I'm begging you to come forward. I have every intention of treating this investigation as a legitimate complaint. Several teams of specialists have already been primed and will descend on the property as soon as the warrant is granted. Please, please consider coming forward to help ensure the search runs smoothly.*

She reread her reply half a dozen times before she hit the Send button. Then she stared at her screen, willing it not to come back, but her heart sank a few seconds later when she received the notification that her email had bounced.

"Damn, shit and blast. What the actual fuck!"

At that moment, Lorne appeared in the doorway. "Hey, bad news. The council told me they lost the key to that place years ago, which is inconceivable." Lorne sighed. "Anyway, I was wondering if you fancied your coffee early. I'm going to make myself one now. Is something wrong?"

Unable to speak in case her anger got the better of her on both counts, Sally gestured for her partner to join her.

Lorne rushed to be by Sally's side and read the email. She squeezed Sally's shoulder and shook her head. "Oh no, he thinks you've ignored his initial contact with you, and you have no way of reassuring him that simply isn't true."

"I know. I tried to respond, but it bounced back. As if I

wasn't feeling bad enough about this already." Sally covered her face with her hands, although she resisted the urge to break down.

"No, Sally. Come on, you need to remain positive. You're not to blame for the hold-up. It's out of our hands. I feel for you, I truly do."

"It's so... so frustrating. I can't remember being in a situation like this before."

"You can't blame yourself. It's the system, it's messed up. Maybe you should issue a formal complaint."

"Do you think that would work? Doing that might endanger our future requests."

"You're probably right. I'd still be tempted to do it, though. It's not right that we should have to wait three days or more to be granted a warrant. How are we supposed to solve a case if we're forced to put up with shit like that all the time?" Lorne growled and returned to the other side of the desk.

Sally smiled at her partner's outburst. "Ignoring that, yes, I'd love a coffee now, thanks."

A dejected Lorne left the office and returned with a mug of coffee and a Penguin biscuit. "I thought you could do with cheering up. Don't eat it all at once."

"Crikey, I haven't had one of these in years!"

"Me neither until Tony picked up a packet the other day."

"Ouch... pick... pick... pick up a Penguin today."

Lorne chuckled. "I remember the ad well. It used to be my favourite biscuit growing up, too."

"And mine. You've got a good man there, Lorne."

"I know. He's the best. I think we both landed on our feet."

They jumped when a loud shout erupted in the office

next door. Lorne dashed out to see what the fuss was about while Sally tidied up the unopened envelopes she hadn't got around to and shoved them in her in-tray for later.

An excited Lorne reappeared in the doorway. "It would seem the wait is over. We've been given the green light, boss."

"That's amazing. I'll grab my coffee, and we'll decide what to do next." A thrill ran through Sally as she collected her mug. Her mind buzzing, she returned to the team. "Joanna, I apologise, but you'll have to stay here and handle the phone calls."

Joanna waved away her apology. "I expected that, boss. I'll probably be more use here anyway. Not sure if I'd be able to cope inside the house."

"It's going to be tough in there. There's no denying that. Everyone else should gather their belongings and come with me and Lorne to the location. I'll give the pathologist a ring and see if she can join us. Hopefully, she's pulled in extra troops to deal with what lies ahead of us." She puffed out her cheeks, took a sip of her coffee and dialled the lab's number from her mobile. "Pauline, I'm glad I've caught you. Can you talk?"

"Providing it's quick. I'm due to meet the family of a victim. What's up?"

"I wanted to let you know that the permission has been granted for Oakridge Hall. We're on our way out there now."

"I'll let SOCO know, and I'll join you as soon as humanly possible. It's good timing. I haven't got any PMs planned for today."

"Great. I'll send you the postcode."

"Don't bother. I took the initiative to do some research on the property when you first mentioned it. See you later."

"Take care." Sally ended the call and let out an enormous sigh. "I can't believe the warrant has finally come through. Now the hard work begins, folks."

Sally, Lorne, Jordan and Stuart left the station a few minutes later and set off in two cars.

"It's at times like this I wish we had a bigger team at our disposal," Sally said. The traffic flowed nicely through Wymondham and, with no roadworks to contend with, the satnav predicted they'd arrive in twenty minutes.

"Nervous?" Lorne asked.

"That would be the understatement of the decade. Let's hope it doesn't take us long to find something."

"I was thinking the same. The longer it takes, the more the doubt is going to set in. There's got to be something there, right? Especially after you received that email today. We should have asked Joanna to trace it."

"I'll mention it later. We're bound to need to get in touch with her before the day is out."

"Talking of which, are we going to be expected to work longer today?"

"Let's see how things progress, first. Bearing in mind that there will be no electricity at the house. I've just had a thought. I should text Pauline and remind her of that. SOCO can ensure they bring a generator with them."

"Makes sense. I hadn't thought about that aspect of things. It means our time could be limited here today until a generator is in place."

"Not something we've had to think about in the past, maybe on the odd occasion."

"I think we'll probably need more than one generator to assist us. This place is enormous."

Sally texted Pauline about the generators they would

need and immediately got a response from the pathologist: *It's all in hand. Stop worrying. P.*

"That told me." She showed the reply to Lorne.

"She's a bugger. It's called keeping you on your toes, Sal."

"She does that all right. Let's see what this place has to offer us, then. I'll see if the boys can get in around the back, through a window, rather than break down that magnificent door."

"I agree. We're going to need to keep this place secure at night to prevent the squatters from moving in."

"You're right. Can you imagine what carnage that would cause if they moved in before we had a chance to search every room?"

Sally shook her head, ridding herself of the image her mind had conjured up. "That would be an absolute disaster. There are enough homeless people around at the moment, thanks to the cost-of-living crisis."

"Yeah, don't go there."

They exited the car, and Sally dished out the protective suits to Lorne and the boys, along with shoe covers and gloves, to complete their ensembles. "Don't put the covers on until we're inside the building. We're going to need to find a way into the property without breaking down the door. Can you lads check every window on the ground floor round the back? Lorne and I will check the ones at the front."

Stuart and Jordan headed around the side of the property.

"I can't see us finding a way in, not after all these years," Lorne said.

"We will need to think positively. Maybe there's a cellar and the boys will stumble across an opening around the back."

"Excellent point and it will save us a lot of hassle if they do."

They split up and alternately checked all the windows they could reach without the aid of a ladder.

"Why did God make us so small?" Sally complained, barely able to reach the bottom of the window, even standing on tiptoes.

"This is ridiculous. We could do with some steps."

"Don't look at me. I carry enough crap in the boot of my car without having to consider bringing a ladder to every scene."

"Might be worth giving Simon a call?" Lorne suggested after another one of her attempts failed.

"Good idea. Hang fire, don't exert your energy more than you have to." Sally rang her husband. "Hi, love, are you busy?"

He laughed. "It depends on what you're about to ask me."

"We've been granted the search warrant and we're at the location now, but silly me, I forgot to bring any steps with us."

"Let me guess, and you were wondering if we had a spare half an hour to help you out."

"Umm... yes, or is that asking too much of my loving husband?"

Simon roared with laughter. "As it happens, we're not too far from there and I'm always prepared, unlike someone I can mention. I have a set of steps in the boot. We'll drop by soon."

"I knew you'd be willing to come to our rescue."

"Get out of here. We'll see you shortly."

"Love you," Sally said and hung up. "Time to assess how the boys are doing out back."

They trotted the length of the front façade and around the side. By that time, they were both out of breath.

"Bloody hell, if the magnitude of the task ahead hadn't dawned on us already, I think it has now." Lorne shook her head. "It's going to take months for us to cover the ground floor alone, let alone the rooms on the first and second floors."

"Try not to think about it. Depending on what we find out of the traps, I think I'll need to have a word with the chief about supplying us with extra manpower. It's going to be a tough ask otherwise."

"One of those enquiries that is likely to piss people off, especially if it takes a while to get going. By that I mean, if we fail to uncover anything inappropriate."

"Let's not think about that for now."

They reached the end of the building and spotted Stuart and Jordan in the distance.

"I'm going to cheat and ring them, save my voice." Sally called Stuart's number. "Hi, we're over to your right." He glanced her way and waved. "How's it going so far?"

"Nothing yet, boss."

"Lorne and I had trouble reaching the windows, short arses that we are. I've called my husband; he's bringing us some steps. What about access to the cellar?"

"We've not come across anything so far, boss. All the windows are either locked or have seized up."

"Okay, keep trying. Give me a shout if you have any luck, we'll be around the front, waiting for Simon to show up." She ended the call, and they wandered back to the front of the building.

"There are barely any windows on this elevation," Lorne pointed out.

"And no access to the cellar. Maybe it hasn't got one."

Lorne scrolled through her phone and showed Sally a black-and-white photo of a fully stocked wine cellar from days gone by.

"Must have been before it was turned into the hospital during the war."

"Yes, the photo was credited to the photographer in 1935."

"I bet it was cleared before it changed hands. If not, can you imagine all those wounded soldiers going for a wander during the night and ending up in the wine cellar?"

Lorne tutted. "Funnily enough, no, I can't imagine that."

Sally pulled a face at her. "I was kidding. Where's your sense of humour gone?"

Lorne pointed at Simon's Range Rover coming through the arched entrance. "Saved by our heroes."

"If only that were true. I'd love to have Simon and Tony working alongside us on this case, wouldn't you?"

"I haven't thought about it before, but now that you've mentioned it, that would be great. We'd have this place searched in no time at all."

Sally raised a hand. "Let's not get carried away. I mean, they're used to approaching renovations with a sledgehammer."

"That's true. Forget I mentioned it."

They met their partners at the front of the building. Simon let Dex out of the car. He trotted over to cock his leg in the area that once upon a time used to be an immaculate lawn. Then he worked his way back to them, and Sally made a fuss of him.

"Hello, boy. I bet you didn't expect to see me on your travels today, did you?"

"This place is amazing," Tony said. He surveyed the area with a gobsmacked expression.

"You're not wrong," Simon agreed. "Don't go getting any ideas. It would take millions, tens of millions even, to put this place back together again. Not to mention the time involved."

"Have you brought the steps?" Sally asked, eager to get on.

"Of course. Have I ever let you down before?"

"There was that time when..." Sally began and laughed when her husband's mouth dropped open. "I'm joking."

"Good job." He went to the boot and withdrew a small set of steps, which he handed to Sally.

Her gaze drifted between the steps and the window to her right. "Is that it?"

Lorne dug her in the ribs and whispered, "Don't be so ungrateful. Thanks, Simon, they look perfect to me."

Sally carried the steps towards the first window and opened them up. They proved adequate, and she peered through the window.

"Going to eat your words now, are you?" Simon teased Sally.

"Sorry. They're great. I'll bring them home this evening."

"Are you dismissing us?" Simon asked. "I was hoping we could have a wander around the grounds."

"Don't go too far, this place will be crawling with tech guys soon, and you really shouldn't be here," Sally shouted as Simon and Tony set off with the ever-enthusiastic Dex bounding behind them.

"Don't worry, we'll be back in ten minutes. It's too good an opportunity to miss having a snoop around," he called back over his shoulder.

"Bloody cheek, and there was me thinking he'd be a gentleman and volunteer to help us gain access," Sally grumbled. She clung on to the rail of the steps as they moved on the uneven gravel.

Lorne came to the rescue and steadied the steps with both hands.

"Thanks, you're a pal."

"My pleasure. Can you see anything?"

"My worst nightmare: the window is covered with decades of cobwebs, making it difficult to see clearly."

"Shit, spiders are my worst nightmare, too."

The gravel crunched behind Sally. She glanced over her right shoulder. "What is it, Jordan?"

"We've gained access to the property through a kitchen window around the back, boss."

"That's great news. I was in danger of suffering from vertigo up here."

The three of them laughed, and Sally reversed down the three steps to terra firma. Once she landed, she brushed herself down to regain her composure. "There's a reason I chose to be a copper over becoming a window cleaner."

They followed Jordan around the side of the house. Out of the corner of her eye, she saw Simon and Tony returning from their exploration.

"I see you've found a way in then," Simon said.

"Yes, we've yet to get inside. Thanks for bringing the steps out. I'll see you at home later."

"In other words, piss off," Simon replied.

Sally grinned. "It's police business, and you shouldn't be here."

Simon slapped a hand over his chest and looked mortified. "Try to do my wife a favour and this is the thanks I get."

"Get out of here." Sally shoved her husband in the back to encourage him on his way.

"But I'm your husband. Sharing is caring and..." he objected light-heartedly.

Sally rolled her eyes. "Haven't you got work to do? Tony, take him away, please."

Simon wailed and vocally objected his way back to the Range Rover, causing Sally yet more embarrassment.

"He's a bloody nightmare. Let's ignore the freak show and get in there. Who's volunteering?"

Jordan and Stuart raised their hands at the same time.

Sally's finger flicked between them as she mumbled her rendition of eeny meeny. "It's you, Stuart."

Jordan high-fived his colleague and wished him good luck.

"Make your way to the front door and get that open ASAP. We'll be waiting around there for you once we've helped to give you a leg up."

"Yes, boss."

Jordan took the brunt of his partner's weight and, between the three of them, they heaved Stuart through the window he had only managed to open halfway.

Sally, Lorne and Jordan raced around the front of the building. At the same time, Simon's Range Rover was turning onto the main road.

"I'm going to get another suit from the car in case Stuart's is damaged." Sally ran back to the vehicle, retrieved the suit and returned to wait with the others. Movement came from the other side of the door.

"Is that furniture being moved?" Lorne tilted her head and asked.

"Sounds like it to me," Jordan agreed. "Are you all right, Stu?"

"Yeah, I'm getting there. We're in luck. I can see a key in

the lock, but someone has stacked a load of furniture against the door. I'm shifting it."

"Okay, be careful. Take your time. We're in no hurry." A sound echoed behind Sally, and two SOCO vans rumbled up the driveway towards them. "Correction, SOCO have arrived. Do you need Jordan to come in there and help you?"

With that, the door opened, and a panting Stuart smiled at them. With sweat beading his brow, he placed his hands on his knees to catch his breath after his exertions.

Sally was the first to enter the building. She patted Stuart on the back. She stared at the collection of heavy chairs and desks strewn around the hallway. "Good job. That's a hell of a lot of furniture to use to barricade the door. Take a break for five minutes while we have a look around."

He stood upright and shook his head. "I'm fine now."

The doors slammed on the vehicles, and four SOCO techs arrived at the bottom of the steps.

"Who is in charge here?" the oldest man asked.

Sally took a step forward. "DI Sally Parker. Thanks for coming so quickly. We gained access through a window around the back, and this is the first time we've entered the building properly. We're all suited and booted."

"I can see that. We'll get the equipment from the vehicles and be with you in a moment or two."

"We'll have a quick nosey around while you do that."

The techs returned to their vehicles.

Lorne and Jordan joined Sally and Stuart in the magnificent hallway. There was a wooden staircase over to the right. A plethora of windows at the front and the back of the building meant the area was flooded with light, despite the cobwebs covering most of them. Sally shuddered at the prospect of coming across enormous spiders at every turn.

"I know what has just gone through that head of yours," Lorne whispered in her ear.

"I can't get them out of my mind."

"You're going to have to if we want to search this place thoroughly."

"The spiders will be more scared of us than we are of them," Jordan added. "Let's face it, they've had the free run of this place for decades."

"That's true," Sally said. "Okay, why don't we split up into our usual pairs and see what we can find? There are a lot of rooms to cover down here. We'll poke our heads in all of them and move on unless we find anything worth investigating further. Got that?"

Stuart and Jordan nodded and set off to check the right side of the property while Lorne and Sally went left, leaving the techs to do their own thing until someone discovered something on their search.

"This place is incredible. It's not as bad as I thought it would be," Lorne said.

"I'm amazed it's in good nick, too. I think it would have been different if the roof was missing or if any major leaks had developed up there."

"That's true. We'll find out soon enough."

They walked through the grand entrance hall and pushed open the door to a room at the front of the property, which turned out to be a library stacked full of colourful books dating back years. Not a modern hardback or paperback in sight.

Lorne whistled, "Wow, I bet there are a few first editions amongst this lot."

"Blimey, I thought the same. Okay, let's keep moving. We can come back and have a better snoop around in here later."

"We might even find a secret passageway."

Sally nodded and backed out of the room. "It wouldn't surprise me. What's in here?"

The next room was a large office which again contained shelves with dozens of multi-coloured books. "I reckon this must have been the headmaster's office, or whatever the person in charge of an establishment like this is called," Sally said.

"Again, we should come back and examine it. I've probably been watching too many films where there always seems to be a secret panel behind one of the bookcases. It's going to be a matter of taking your pick around here."

"You're not wrong. Okay, let's move on. We've got plenty to discover yet."

They came across several classrooms next, and finally, after working their way back through the house, they arrived in the kitchen. The window, which Stuart had climbed through, was still open. The entire room was like something out of a time warp, with no modern furniture in sight. All the units appeared to be handmade and were freestanding with oak worktops. A rack hung from the ceiling; on it were dozens of sieves and colanders of various sizes.

Off the kitchen was a large pantry, still filled with tinned food.

Sally opened a few of the cupboards, and several spiders scurried back to their webs in the corners. "Yuck, bloody things. It would appear the boys wouldn't have gone hungry unless all this was for the staff's benefit."

"More than likely. I'm guessing some of this stuff would sell for a lot of money at an auction house."

"Let's not go there. Fancy the council leaving it to rot. I'll never be able to work them out. This place could have been made into something really special, and they've chosen to ignore it all these years."

"Mind-blowing, isn't it? Bloody idiots."

The door opened, and Stuart and Jordan appeared.

"Found anything of interest?" Sally asked.

"That side of the house comprised a storeroom, a couple of classrooms, what appears to be a staffroom and toilets. There's a conservatory at the end, overlooking the garden on that side of the house, which has a view of the lake."

Sally nodded. "Might be worth seeing if there's anything at the bottom of that lake, in the future. Let's concentrate on the inside of the house for now."

"Do you want us to start in the upstairs rooms, boss?" Jordan asked.

"Yes. Lorne and I will come with you."

The four of them left the kitchen and began the long journey up the winding staircase to the floor above.

Sally spotted another small staircase leading up to the last floor at the end of the hallway. "Why don't you boys take the next floor up and see what's on offer up there?"

They nodded and set off, eager to explore.

"Rather them than me," Lorne said. "To my mind, the further you get into the roof space of a house, the eerier it gets."

"That's why I suggested we search this level. You go left and I'll go right. We'll get this completed quicker if we split up."

"Fine with me."

Sally checked the first couple of rooms, which were huge and had around ten beds in each of them. She met up with Lorne in the hallway. "All bedrooms, right?"

"Yep, with between eight and ten beds in each of them. One room was smaller than the others."

"On we go then."

The next room Sally came to turned out to be a huge bathroom, with four cubicles on each side. She stepped into the room and pushed open each of the cubicles. Thankfully, they were all empty. They had old-fashioned cisterns high above the toilets. There was a faint smell of the sewers backing up. "To be expected," she said.

Sally left the room and continued her search. She counted another five doors ahead of her.

She popped her head into the first room, which turned out to be a large linen cupboard, and then moved on. The following four rooms were all smaller bedrooms, housing between four and six metal-framed beds.

Lorne joined her and reported that the rooms on the other side of the hallway were virtually the same as the ones she'd been in.

Stuart and Jordan met them as they approached the staircase leading up to the next level.

"Nothing up there except six rooms, each with four beds. One room had a attic access, but I didn't have a nosey up there. I'll go back if you want me to?" Jordan said.

"No, it's fine. We'll leave it for now. Neither of us has found anything untoward so far. Let's go back downstairs, and I'll have a chat with the techs and see what they suggest we do next."

"We could check the grounds, boss," Stuart proposed.

"Okay, you do that. Stay quite close to the house."

The four of them made their way back along the corridor to the ground floor. The techs were bringing in their equipment. Sally peered out of the front door as Pauline's van arrived.

"Come on, we'll have a chat with Pauline while she gets ready."

Pauline drew the van to a halt alongside the SOCO vehicles and stepped out. She seemed harassed, and Sally cringed as she approached the pathologist.

"Hi, thanks for coming so promptly. How are you?"

"Eager to get on. Aware of what a daunting task lies ahead of me, or should I say us? How come you're looking so chirpy?"

Sally shrugged. "I wasn't aware that I was. A member of my team gained access through the kitchen window. All the furniture in the hallway was barricading the door."

"Anything else I should know?"

"We've had a quick nosey in all the rooms. There are three floors in total."

"Shit. Go on."

"The one room that caught my eye was the library."

"You're thinking secret panels in that room, am I right?"

"Correct. Plus, in the main office, there's another bookshelf which might be worth a gander."

"Feel free to have a tinker and let us know if you find anything," Pauline shot back quickly.

"We don't mind. We can start on that straight away. Umm... there's a lake on the side of the property that might be worth investigating further."

"If we find anything in the house, I'll make the call then and get a dive team out here. Let's see how we go for now."

"Whatever you think is for the best. Have you got specific equipment that will detect if there are any bodies buried behind the walls?"

Pauline raised an eyebrow at Sally and turned to look at Lorne. "Is she for real?"

Lorne put a hand over her mouth. Sally could tell she was suppressing a giggle.

"Simple question," Sally replied.

"I'm teasing. Leave the intricacies of endeavours to us. I tend not to interfere with your job, so I'd like you to offer us the same courtesy."

"That told me," Sally mumbled. "Okay, we'll leave you to it and return to the library. We'll give you a shout if we find anything."

"You do that." Pauline opened the back of her van, effectively dismissing any further conversation between them.

Sally and Lorne returned to the house and entered the hallway.

"She can be so bloody rude at times," Sally grumbled.

"You're taking it to heart. She's keen to get on with her job. Stop being so sensitive."

"She's not the best person to deal with, but there are ways of talking to people. I always feel on tenterhooks when I speak to her."

Lorne rubbed her upper arm. "Try not to worry about her. We have bigger fish to fry."

"Yeah, you're right, as usual. Let's crack on."

They weaved their way past the furniture, and someone tutted behind them. Pauline had entered the hallway. Lorne gave Sally a slight nudge in the back to get her moving again, away from a possible confrontation between the two of them.

Once they were out of earshot, Sally said, "What did she expect? I warned her what it would be like inside."

Lorne shook her head. "Leave it. You're working yourself up into a state for nothing. It's not worth the aggro, love. Come on, we've got a job to do."

They entered the library first. Again, they split up so they could check the room over quickly.

"What are we searching for? Have you ever come across a hidden panel before?" Lorne asked.

"Nope, I'm as much in the dark as you are. Maybe a small lever at the side of a panel. Should we move some of the books in the hope there's a button behind one of them?" Sally glanced out of the window; Stuart and Jordan were on their way back to the house. She knocked on the glass and gestured for the two men to join them.

Lorne ran to the door and waited for them to appear in the hallway. "Down here, lads."

"Wow, this is amazing," Jordan said when they entered the room.

"It is. We need your help to search for a secret panel. Lorne and I will take this side of the room while you two search the other. Check everything, every nook and cranny, and move every book if you have to."

The four of them began their search, and it was a good twenty minutes before Jordan shouted, "I've got something! The panel moved when I pulled this book forward."

They all gathered around to watch Jordan pull on the panelling. It appeared to be jammed, so Stuart, being the tallest, tugged the top while Jordan yanked hard on the bottom shelves. The door shifted a little but got stuck after a few inches.

"We could do with a crowbar or something to get in there," Lorne suggested.

Sally ran out of the room and back to the car. She opened the boot, removed a crowbar and returned to the library, slightly out of breath. "Here you go. Try this."

Stuart took the bar and anchored it between the two sections of the bookcase. "Don't blame me if I cause any damage. I reckon the wood has warped over the years."

"Don't worry about it, just get it open, Stu."

Lorne and Sally helped tug at the shelving and, within a few minutes, the door sprang open.

"Thank God for that and with minimal damage, too. Well done, Stu." Sally patted him on the back, and his cheeks reddened.

"All in a day's work," he said and laughed.

"Now all we have to do is get in there and have a snoop around. Not something I'm looking forward to doing."

"I don't mind going in there," Jordan volunteered.

Sally grinned. "I was hoping you'd say that."

"I'll go with him," Stuart said.

Sally nodded and then wished them both good luck. Lorne shone the torch from her phone into the darkness, guiding Stuart and Jordan's way. They withdrew their phones and did the same.

"God, it stinks in here. Musty, and there's another smell that I'm struggling to identify," Jordan said.

"Shit! What's that?" Stuart screeched.

"Two rats. They're big buggers, too."

"Christ, I'm glad we didn't take the plunge to go first," Lorne said. "I would have died on the spot if I'd encountered one of them."

"And I would have ended up lying on the floor next to you," Sally replied. "What else is in there?"

"There are a couple of doors. I'm going to open the first one now. There's a key in the door," Stuart said.

Sally held her crossed fingers up and closed her eyes.

"Holy shit! Oh God, I can't believe what I'm seeing..." Stuart said.

He reappeared in the doorway; the redness in his cheeks had disappeared. "Jesus, there are human remains in there. They're shackled to the wall, boss."

Tempted as she was to get in there and see for herself, the thought of coming face to face with a large critter stopped her. "Okay, let's close it again and get SOCO in here."

Lorne left the room and returned with Pauline a few minutes later.

"You're unashamedly afraid of a few rats, I hear," Pauline said and brushed past Sally.

Sally shot Lorne one of her how-could-you-betray-me-like-that looks. Lorne shrugged, and they waited for Pauline to emerge again.

"We need to start here. The rats could come this way once we start messing around in their playground, so it's up to you whether you stick around."

"We can take a hint. Have you checked the other rooms in there?"

"I have, and I discovered the same. Three bodies, all youngsters."

"Shit! Not what I wanted to hear," Sally said. "Okay, we're going to leave you to it. This is the only opening we've found. We've searched extensively in here. There's another bookcase in the main office. We'll head in there and check that out."

"Wise move. Let me know if, or should I say when, you find something. I doubt if this is the only secret room in a property of this size."

"I'm thinking the same." Sally led the team out of the library and into what might have been the headmaster's office.

They searched from one end of the bookcase to the other several times, high and low, but found nothing.

Sally exhaled a relieved sigh. "That's good. I hope we don't stumble upon anything else unsettling after what we found in the library."

"God, it doesn't bear thinking about, does it? Maybe we

should get the divers in ASAP," Lorne suggested. "What did you find in the grounds, boys?"

"There were two wooden huts, mainly filled with gardening equipment, and a few metal barns, probably dating back to the war. They were packed with excess furniture, school desks and stacks of chairs," Jordan replied.

"We also discovered what appeared to be an air-raid shelter. It was locked. We didn't break down the door to investigate further because you told us not to be too long," Stuart added.

"I dread to think what we'll find in there." Sally puffed out her cheeks. Her mind racing, she shook her head. "Where the heck do we begin? I doubt if they are going to be the last bodies we find on site."

"Kids, as well. I can't believe it," Lorne said. "Didn't they have parents? If that were true, why didn't they forcibly enter the house to find out where their children were? This is all so wrong, and what's more frustrating is the lack of media coverage or such like that we've come across."

"Why kill the kids? Who killed them? Why would they feel the need to torture them before their deaths? How was this allowed to happen? Where were the authorities in all of this? The reports of missing children? It's mind-boggling what we've uncovered so far and what might be ahead of us."

"Maybe you should ask Pauline if she's got in touch with other teams working in the area or possibly in Suffolk. If we don't get extra help, this investigation could last until next Christmas," Lorne pointed out.

Sally chewed on her lip. "With resources cut to a minimum, who's going to fund a massive job like this?"

"Have a word with Pauline first. See what she's arranged and go from there."

Sally cringed and lowered her voice to ask, "I don't suppose you'd be up for doing that for me, would you?"

Lorne shook her head. "You're nuts. The more you distance yourself from her, the more strained your relationship will become. I thought you guys had met an understanding and agreed to start over."

"We had, sort of. I know you probably think I'm being silly, but all I'm trying to do is keep the peace on this one."

"All right, I'll do it. Wish me luck."

"Good luck. We'll be outside. I'm in desperate need of fresh air."

"Okay, I'll catch you all up."

Sally, Jordan and Stuart exited the building, but Lorne stayed behind to talk to Pauline. Outside, Sally walked to the end of the property and stared towards the lake. *I'm sensing something is in there. I'm not prepared to wait for Pauline to make the call, we need to get the divers sorted before we do anything else.* So that's what she did. She called the station and asked Joanna for the dive team's number.

"How's it going out there, boss?"

"We've found four bodies already. I think that number is going to increase before long, too. Can you get the dive team out here ASAP, Joanna? There's an enormous lake here, and my gut instinct tells me that there are possibly more bodies in it."

Joanna tutted. "Shit! That's not good. I'll organise the dive team if that's what you want. Sounds like you have enough on your plate out there as it is."

"Thanks, love. I appreciate it. Let me know what they say."

Lorne joined them a few moments later. She seemed down in the mouth, and Sally braced herself for bad news.

"Well? What did she say?"

"She's tried her best. There might be a couple of techs spare. They're travelling up from Suffolk, but that's about all. I think that's why she's pissed off. She's realised what a massive task this is going to be, and she hasn't got the staff needed to deal with it."

"In other words, I need to give her a break, right?"

Lorne smiled. "I would, if I were in your shoes. How did it go with the dive team?"

"Joanna suggested she should organise that for us at her end. I'm waiting for a call back from her."

"You sound down. Are you all right?"

"I suppose I'm feeling shell-shocked. We have the responsibility of transferring the baton to Pauline and her team. It's a weird feeling. I want to be here to help them, but I'm also reticent about being here and discovering more bodies."

"Because of the age of the victims?" Lorne asked.

Sally nodded. "Yep. I'm always the same where victims of this age are concerned. Why take a child's life? I've always put it down to cowardice, and nothing anyone says will change that."

"I know. It's a tough part of the job. Not something I've had to deal with that often, thank goodness, apart from the atrocities that were uncovered in the investigation Charlie was involved in as a teenager. A few of the young girls didn't make it. They died whilst men in their fifties and sixties were having sex with them."

"Oh no, please don't tell me any more, Lorne. That must have been horrendous for you, an utter nightmare situation to deal with."

"It was. Which is why I insisted I wanted to remain on the case."

"And was the cause behind your fall out with Sean Roberts and your superintendent at the time?"

"Correct. When something that personal happens, you can't possibly understand the trauma, the utter desperation involved. I had to dig deeper than I've ever dug before, and all this after losing my beloved partner."

Sally wrapped her arms around Lorne when the tears filled her eyes. Stuart and Jordan moved away from them and walked back towards the house.

"I'm sorry, love. There's no disputing that you and your family had a really tough time back then. It's important for you to remind yourself of the positives that came out of that case."

Lorne took a step back out of her grasp and frowned. "What positives?"

"Oh God, that Charlie survived for a start."

"I know, I do regularly. I shouldn't keep going over and over old ground. Things that happened nearly twenty years ago now. It's not like I can change anything, is it?"

"No. However, you're entitled to feel reflective. You lost a few people around that time, Pete and Jacques. Didn't your sister, Jade, get kidnapped around then, as well?"

"Yes, but during another case." Lorne inhaled a few large breaths and shook her arms out. "But this isn't about me. To our knowledge, so far, we have four children who have lost their lives. The question is, are we ever going to know who they were?"

"Not unless Pauline is prepared to use a forensic anthropologist to reconstruct their faces. If no one has reported their kids missing over the years, is it going to be worth it, you know, when resources are as tight as they are?"

"Good point. What a bloody mess. I can feel my frustration already growing with this one, and we're still only in the preliminary stages."

A tech came running out of the house, down the steps towards one of the SOCO vans.

"Come on, we'd better see what's going on." Sally tugged Lorne's forearm, and together they raced over to the van. "Have you found something else in there?" Sally asked.

"Yes, we think so. I was checking the walls in the pantry, and one side sounded hollow, as though there was something behind it. I smashed through; a single brick wall had been erected, and behind it was another room."

"Oh God, please tell me you haven't found more bodies?"

"No, but more importantly, and I don't mean that disrespectfully, we've uncovered what appears to be a secret office."

Sally frowned. "There must be a doorway to it somewhere then, right?"

"Nope. My colleague and I have concluded that the room was blocked up on purpose, possibly to bury what lies within."

"Shit! Really? This might be what we need to continue the investigation and prevent it from grinding to a halt before it has a chance to get underway."

"Correct. I'm just getting some equipment, and then we're intending to remove the bricks, one by one."

"Can my men help with that task?"

"If you can spare them. We've got such a lot to cover in there, and we're sinking fast without the extra hands to help us."

"Consider it done." Sally turned and shouted across the driveway, "Stuart, Jordan, they've discovered another room inside and could do with some extra help for an hour or two. Can you lend them a hand?"

"Sure thing, boss."

They walked towards the SOCO van to assist the tech with taking the equipment needed.

Sally's mobile rang. She stepped away to answer it. "Hi, Joanna. Any news for me?"

"We're in luck. The dive team is available. I've given them your location. They should be with you within half an hour."

Sally let out a relieved sigh. "That's great news. Thanks for sorting that out for us, love."

"Dare I ask how things are going there?"

"They're going, slowly. We've just heard that a secret office has been found. As soon as we can get in there, we will."

"Wow, that sounds promising. It's not like we have much else to go on right now."

"You took the words out of my mouth. Keep digging at your end."

"I will. Speak later, boss."

Sally hung up and faced Lorne to share the good news. "They'll be here within thirty minutes."

"Great news. Things appear to be coming together at last, Sal."

She held up her crossed fingers.

3

An hour later, Sally and Lorne were standing alongside the lake, overseeing the dive team's operation while sharing a ham and cheese sandwich that Jordan had nipped out to buy from a nearby shop.

The secret office inside the building was now fully accessible. Sally left the boys to deal with that because she was determined to go with her gut instinct and remain by the lake, just in case.

"How are you feeling, or is that a daft question?" Lorne asked.

Sally took a swig of water from her bottle then said, "I'm okay. No, I lied, I'm on tenterhooks. My anxiety will ease once they've thoroughly examined the place and chosen to end their search."

"You know it could take them a couple of days to complete the task, don't you? It'll be murky as hell down there."

"Yeah, I'm aware of the problems they are likely to encounter, hence my fingers being crossed all the time. Even though I'm finding that really uncomfortable at the moment."

Lorne kicked out at a large piece of gravel. It plopped into the water, and it rippled. "This is so boring. Please, guys, do us a favour and find something soon."

"Patience. It'll happen, I'm sure. If all else fails, we've got the secret office to search through. I think I'll ring Stuart to see how they're getting on in there." Sally withdrew her phone from her pocket. "Stuart, how's it going?"

"Interesting discovery, boss. I reckon it's going to take us weeks to sift through it all, though."

"Interesting in what way?"

"We've got names galore at our disposal."

"Wow, that's brilliant news. We'll hang around out here for a while longer and then come and find you."

"There's no rush. I don't think this will be a quick job."

She ended the call and stared at the expansive lake, willing a diver to break through the surface. It didn't happen. There was a bench over to the right. "We might as well take a seat."

"It'll probably be wet through and covered in moss. I think I'd rather stand."

"Yeah, I never thought about that." Sally puffed out her cheeks. "I hate all this waiting around. I'm not the most patient person in the world."

"No shit, Sherlock."

"Sorry, is that me spouting the obvious?"

"Somewhat. Wait, the diver has resurfaced."

They raced around to the side of the lake where the diver had surfaced. He was talking to the man in charge, who was scratching his head as he listened.

They came to a standstill close to the two men.

"Something wrong?" Sally asked.

The diver glanced at his boss, who had a name tag around his neck, Trevor Lockart, but said nothing.

"Yes, there's something down there. We don't want to move it yet."

Sally frowned. "Can you give us a clue?"

"There's what appears to be a sack; it's heavy, as though it has been weighted down with rocks," the diver replied.

"How big is the sack? Large enough to hold a body?"

The diver glanced at his boss a second time and then at Sally. "Yes."

Sally thumped her thigh. "I knew it. Knew there would be something down there. Fuck! Sorry for my language."

"Hey, don't be. We've heard a darn sight worse than that over the years."

"So, what happens next?"

"I'm going to ring another crew and ask them if they can join us. I'd get in there myself, but I'm still recovering from a broken leg. The doctor has advised me not to get in the water for a couple of months, especially something this dirty, in case my wound gets infected."

"That's understandable. How did you break it?" Sally asked, intrigue getting the better of her.

"On a skiing trip. Right, let me ring my mate. I'll get back to you in a moment." He returned to his vehicle, and the diver bobbed around on the surface.

"Is the visibility crap down there? I noticed you had a light on during your search."

"This is one of the worst locations I've been to in a while. Lakes are always a nightmare to trawl through because of the stagnant water. In a river, you've got a constant flow happening, so it doesn't allow things to become stagnant."

Sally nodded. "I'm with you. I hadn't thought about it

like that before. We really appreciate all that you're doing for us."

"Don't mention it. It's all in a day's work."

"Even if some days are better than others, eh?"

The diver nodded.

His boss returned. "Okay, Sid and Alan are on their way over here. Get out, Pat. We might as well wait for them to arrive. They shouldn't be long."

"We're going to leave you to it. There's something we need to see inside the building. We'll be back in a while," Sally informed them.

"Take your time. We'll be around for a day or two yet."

"That long? Do you think you're going to find anything else down there?"

"It's possible. I've only searched a small section of the lake so far," the diver said.

"Crikey! Okay, thanks, guys. We'll come back soon."

Sally and Lorne marched back to the house, eager to see what was happening inside. Before they entered, they covered their shoes with new protective booties. They wound their way past the furniture cluttering the hallway, but Sally stopped when she overheard voices coming from a room on the right.

"Let's take a peep."

They entered the room to find two techs and Pauline staring at a hole that had been made in one wall of what used to be a classroom. The rustling of their suits alerted Pauline that they were behind her.

"What have you found now?" Sally asked.

"Looks like another secret room. We're deciding how to proceed."

Sally took a step forward. "Can I have a peek?"

Pauline and the two techs on either side of her stepped

away, allowing her access to the hole they had created in the wall.

Tentatively, Sally peered through the opening and immediately took a step back. "What the actual fuck?"

Lorne was eager to have a look and said something similar. "Effing hell. What else are we going to uncover in this sodding place?"

"You tell me," Pauline said.

Sally covered her face with her hands. Despite feeling overwhelmed by what she had seen, her curiosity pushed her to take another look. She approached the opening, and this time remained there to survey it. "Jesus, it's like something from the Dark Ages."

"You're not wrong," Lorne admitted. "Was that equipment used on the boys, or the patients when it was a hospital? That's the question."

"Now that is an excellent question," Pauline said. "It's going to be difficult to tell. We don't know when the room was built."

"Are you going to be able to find out?" Sally enquired.

"Possibly. If we can find an expert who can identify the materials that were used, but that's a long shot. Something we can deal with going forward."

"Bloody sickening. This is turning out to be a house of horrors," Sally said.

"It's undoubtedly the worst crime scene I've had to attend during my career, and we haven't even scratched the surface yet. We've still got two floors above to tackle," Pauline complained.

"I don't envy you, Pauline. If we can be of help, don't be afraid to ask."

"Hopefully, the other team from Suffolk will arrive soon.

I'll get them to make a start on the rooms upstairs. That'll ease it for us, initially."

"And all this because of a letter," Sally muttered. "This property has stood empty for decades with secret upon secret hidden behind the walls. Someone knew about these rooms and what was going on here."

"Yeah, may they rot in Hell," Lorne added.

"I agree. There's been a huge cover-up going on here for years. Let's hope the office the boys are sifting through now comes up with some answers for us. If only the author of that letter would come forward and speak with me," Sally said. She shook her head and sighed, expressing her frustration.

"There's no point dwelling on that, Sal," Lorne said. "We need to be thankful that this person got in touch with you in the first place, otherwise all this would have remained undiscovered. At least we can do something about it now."

"After fifty years, Lorne? Who the fuck will still be around for the families to seek the justice they need for the victims who have perished at the hands inhumane people?"

Pauline tapped Sally on the shoulder and gestured with her thumb for them to move. "Come on, ladies, out of the way now. We're eager to get on."

"Sorry, yes. Guilty of assessing the situation and thinking out loud. We'll call back and see you soon."

"We're not going anywhere," Pauline shouted after them as they left the room.

"Bloody hell. What the fuck have we uncovered here?" Sally said.

"It's horrific, and in such beautiful surroundings, too. What those kids or patients must have gone through once the door was closed, shutting out the big wide world..."

"Yep, let's not go there. I'm struggling to get my damn

head around this, and I'm betting what we've uncovered so far is just the tip of the iceberg."

"Yeah, I think you're right. There's also what has been found in the lake to consider."

Sally sighed again. "And there could be more bodies out there. My mind feels like a tornado is swirling inside it."

"You're not alone. I'm willing to wager that this will be one of the most complicated cases we'll ever come across."

"Maybe I should make the chief aware of what we've discovered before we go any further."

"It wouldn't hurt to give him a brief update at this stage."

"You check on the boys. I'll go outside and call him." Sally rang the station and asked to be put through to DCI Green's office. Lyn answered. "Hi, Lyn. Sorry to disturb you. Is there any chance I can have a quick chat with the chief, please?"

"Hold on, let me check. He completed another call just a minute ago. I'll be right back."

Sally walked up and down the steps until the secretary came back on the line.

"Hello, Inspector. I'm putting you through to him now."

"You're amazing. Thank you."

"Hello, Inspector Parker. What can I do for you?"

"Hello, sir. I wanted to keep you informed about the current status of the investigation we're involved in."

"Go on. Are you talking about the Oakridge Hall case?"

"That's right. I have some shocking news to tell you."

"Sounds ominous. I take it you've found a body on the premises?"

"Four, possibly five at this point. It's going to take us weeks, if not months, to check every inch of this place. We've already discovered two secret rooms. I've got a dive team here, and they've found what looks to be a body weighted down in a sack at the bottom of the lake. That's yet to be confirmed."

"Jesus, seriously? My God, who would have thought it? What do you need? I'll see if I can get it for you."

"Extra bodies out here. Professionals. I'd rather not have the place swarming with uniformed officers... hang on, scratch that. It might be an idea if half a dozen of them could be spared to search the grounds. Our team found an inaccessible air-raid shelter among the many outbuildings."

"Goodness me. I'm not saying I don't trust you, but I think I should come and see for myself what you're having to deal with out there."

"I agree with you. It's hard to put into words what we're up against here."

"In that case, expect to see me in thirty minutes. I'm going to need to reschedule some of my calls first."

"We'll see you soon, sir."

SALLY'S NERVES were on high alert as she waited for DCI Green to arrive.

"I can tell you're nervous. You're chewing the skin around your fingers," Lorne whispered as they stood on the steps outside.

"I can't help it. Since when does he show up at a crime scene?"

"I wouldn't be quick to jump to conclusions. Maybe he's coming out here to show you some support. It's not unheard of for DCIs to do that, you know."

Sally raised an eyebrow. "Not this DCI. It's highly unusual for him to drop by to see me in the line of duty."

The chief's Audi entered the driveway and headed towards them.

"Shit. Here he is now." She cast a glance sideways at the lake. The divers' colleagues had recently joined them, and two of them were at present submerged under the water. "My major concern is that he'll interfere and start pissing people off, like Pauline and the divers. You know as well as I do that the atmosphere tends to change when a DCI is on site."

Lorne tutted and mumbled, "Honestly, I think you're guilty of overthinking things. He's here now. I'll leave you to it and see how Stuart and Jordan are getting on."

"Gee, thanks. I was hoping I could count on you for moral support."

"Not this time. TTFN." Lorne opened the front door just as DCI Green came up the steps towards Sally. "Afternoon, sir. Nice to see you here."

"Is it? Well, you'd better show me around, Inspector. I'm intrigued to see for myself what you and your team have discovered."

"Where would you prefer to start? Inside or out?"

His gaze drifted up to the thick grey clouds rolling through above them. "Maybe outside would be better, judging by what's in store for us."

"If that's what you want, sir. The other dive team arrived about ten minutes ago. They didn't hang around; they got changed and went into the water straight away. They're down there now."

"Three divers? Is that it? For a lake this size?"

"That's it. It's the cutbacks, sir. We're all impacted by them, either directly or indirectly."

"You don't have to tell me. I've been on the phone twice to the Super today, pleading for more money to cover the potential drain of what little funds we have when a massive task like this lands on our doorstep." He sighed. "It's like getting blood out of a stone."

"Something has got to give, sir. Otherwise, we won't be able to give this case the attention it deserves."

He raised a hand, sensing her frustration. "I'm in your corner and I will continue to fight, if that's what it takes."

"Is that why you've come out here to check on me? To make sure I'm not wasting funds?"

He cocked an eyebrow. "An unnecessary comment, Inspector. If I didn't trust you, you wouldn't be a member of my team. Have I made myself clear?"

Sally's cheeks warmed under his gaze. She'd opened her mouth instead of engaging her brain first. "I apologise, sir."

"Accepted. Don't let it happen again. Now, let's see what the divers are up to, shall we?"

Trevor was using a gadget to observe the divers' movements beneath the water. He showed them the images of the sack they had found earlier. Sally fought hard not to shudder.

"Are you going to bring it up?" DCI Green asked.

"In time, sir. We're having a good look around down there first, then it will turn from a search into a recovery mission."

"Far be it for me to tell you how to do your job. I suppose another couple of hours in the water aren't going to matter, not after all these years."

"That was our thinking, too. It's often more productive to leave something undisturbed and keep searching."

"We'll leave you to it then," Green said.

They turned to walk away, but out of the corner of her eye, Sally noticed a diver surface in the far corner of the lake. His thumb rose.

"Yep, you've guessed it. They've found something else down there."

The three of them rushed to where the diver was dragging himself out of the lake.

"What is it, Pat?" Sally asked.

"Similar to the first sack we found, around thirty feet from it, umm... there are two more sacks."

Sally gasped and shook her head. "Shit! How many more are down there? This is getting ridiculous, and it's pissing me off that we're the ones who are finding these sacks, or possible bodies after all these damn years. It's just not right, is it?"

"While I concur, Inspector, all we can do is make up for previous neglect. We can conduct a thorough search inside and outside the house and see what horrors we uncover. If only to give the victims a proper burial."

Sally and the divers all nodded.

"Come on, Sally, let's leave these good men to continue their excellent work," Green said. "You can take me on a tour of the house. Show me what else you've revealed during your time on site."

On their journey back to the house, he paused to face her and said, "I appreciate how distressing this investigation must be for you and your team, but please, for the sake of the victims and the members of their families who are still alive, you're going to need to suppress any emotion welling up inside you, at least for now."

"We're trying, believe me. However, the more we uncover, the worse it gets. There's no telling where or when this is likely to end, or if we'll ever find all the poor souls who have perished here. I think that's the crux of it and why our emotions are stirred up, because finding one body is always a tough task to deal with, but here, we've discovered... Christ, I've already lost count, five or six up to this point."

He laid a hand on her forearm. "You're doing your best in extenuating circumstances. I repeat, I haven't come out here to ensure you're doing your job properly, anything but, in fact. I could sense how overwhelmed you were on the phone and wanted to give you some extra support. You've got this. If I had any doubts that you were the right person for the job, you wouldn't be here right now."

"Thank you for your kind words, sir. We have no idea where this will end, but at some stage, my team and I are going to have to leave the site and get on with the other side of the investigation. I think it's that which is causing my anxiety levels to escalate. Knowing that the victims died fifty-odd years ago."

"I see what you're getting at. You're worried that the perpetrators might be dead themselves by now."

Sally sighed and glanced back at the house. "Who'd have thought that such a grand location as this could hold such terrors for the victims? I bet the children who attended this school lived in abject terror, fearing they would be the next to die."

"God, don't say that. Do you think they knew their fellow pupils had been killed?"

Sally shrugged. "Who knows? Now I'm even more determined to find the person who wrote that letter to me. What a life he must have lived, knowing that his friends' lives might have ended here."

"It doesn't bear thinking about, does it? Still, all we can do is our best to right the wrongs that have taken place here, over the years, and lay the victims to rest in proper graves. You are eventually going to have to hand the site over to the professionals."

"I agree, if only to keep our sanity intact."

He smiled and nodded. "Show me what else you've uncovered."

First, they made a stop at her car, and both put on clean protective suits. She provided him with gloves and shoe covers.

"It's been a long time since I've had to wear this type of ensemble. How do I look?" He surprised her by giving her a twirl.

She laughed. "Not out of place at all, sir. It suits you."

"Very droll," he said. "It's good to see you smiling again, Sally. I know how difficult the last couple of days have been for you, but you must look to the future and seek justice for the victims."

"Thanks for the pep talk, sir."

Sally led the way through the house and gave the chief a running commentary of the order in which things had occurred since their arrival.

They paused at what the SOCO guys were now calling the 'torture room'.

"What the fuck? And you believe that the young boys at this school experienced whatever took place in here?"

"There's no telling if that's the case or not, sir. Don't forget, this house was also a makeshift hospital during the war. This setup might have been created for the patients' benefit."

"I find both scenarios incredibly hard to digest. Maybe the equipment was brought in from somewhere else to act as a deterrent."

A tech sprayed Luminol over the restraints on the rack. It instantly showed that there was blood on the equipment.

"Sickening," the chief muttered.

"If it's causing our stomachs to churn, then what type of

person do we think would have instigated such a reign of terror and extreme cruelty? How could anyone allow it to happen?"

"I've seen enough in here. Keep up the good work," the chief told the technician and exited the room.

It was Sally's turn to check on her boss. "Are you all right, sir?"

"Ask me that when we move off site. It's the images conjured up by such a macabre find. Oh God... oh shit!"

Sally frowned. "What are you thinking?" She paused, and her mind also started focusing on warped images.

"Are you thinking the same thing?"

"Possibly. That the instruments of torture were to do with sex games?"

"That's unbelievably sick to even contemplate that happening here."

Sally sighed and shrugged. "Anything is possible." She ran a hand over her face and then covered her eyes, trying her best to block out the images that had been stirred up.

"Okay, again, let's park that information on one side and move on. Where is your partner and the rest of your team?"

"Around. I'll show you what else we've discovered. Don't worry, it's not as macabre as this room."

"I'm delighted to hear that. Lead on."

Sally wound her way past the clutter of furniture in the hallway to the kitchen.

"This looks like something out of *Upstairs, Downstairs*."

"Not heard of that one before, sir. I thought it resembled the kitchens from *Downton Abbey*, myself."

"Yes, yes, that's what I meant. Sorry for the confusion."

Sally sniggered and took him into the pantry where the other secret room had been found.

"Goodness me. Hello, people. Don't let us interrupt you. Carry on regardless."

Lorne, Stuart and Jordan all glanced up from the ledgers and journals they were sifting through to acknowledge them and then got back to work.

"All this will take some time to sort through," Green said. "Will you transfer it to the station, Inspector?"

"That's the plan, sir. We don't want to be on site any longer than necessary. Have you found anything of importance yet, Lorne?"

Lorne picked up an A4 journal and opened it to show them a particular page. "We've got a list of names here. Judging by the DOB, also listed, we believe this might be a list of the victims."

"What? That's excellent news. Wait a second, what do you believe these letters represent in the last column here? Or am I being naïve here?"

"M we think might mean the boy was logged as missing, and the K—" Lorne said.

"The K means the boy was killed," Sally finished for her.

"Oh fuck! That's horrendous," the chief said. "Good work, team. There's a reason you guys were selected to head up the Cold Case Team."

Everyone turned his way and either smiled or nodded.

"What else have you stumbled across?" Sally, intrigued to find out, forgot for a moment that her boss was standing beside her.

"This has been the most significant find so far. Stuart has just got his hands on a book with a list of names and certain 'donations'."

Sally and the chief looked at each other and frowned.

"Donations?" Sally asked.

"Yeah. It's something that I'm guessing will become clearer the more we dig," Lorne said.

"After the thoughts the chief and I have conjured up in the 'torture room', I can guess where this is leading."

Lorne frowned and, as the realisation dawned, she cursed, then apologised. "Sorry."

The chief waved away her apology. "I've heard worse over the years, Sergeant. Keep up the good work in here."

He left the room, and Sally followed him through the house back to the main door, although he had to check with her a couple of times to ensure he was going in the right direction.

"I can understand what a challenge this is going to be for you, Inspector. I'll go back to the station, pass on the information to the Super and see if he can find some extra funding from somewhere."

"I think it's important, especially for this investigation, sir. There's no telling where it's going to lead."

"I agree. Don't worry, you have my full backing." He shook her hand, which surprised her.

"You might want to remove your protective suit before driving off, sir."

"Ah yes. That's a good point. Where shall I put it?"

"Leave it with me. I'll get that sorted for you."

He rested a hand on the stony exterior of the building to remove the shoe covers and then slipped out of the suit and snapped off his gloves. Sally bundled them all together, waved him off and returned inside. She dumped the chief's suit in a bag in the corner of the hallway and made her way through the house to join the rest of the team.

"There, that wasn't as bad as you expected, was it?" Lorne asked.

"No. All credit to him, he was really nice. I've got some

sad news for you, though. The divers have found yet another sack in the lake."

"Shit! I'm not surprised, though. If the murderers thought to throw one body in there, I had an inkling it would only be a matter of time before they found more."

"Have you found any personnel documentation?" Sally asked.

"I'm sure we will, eventually. This lot will take at least the rest of the week to go through."

"We should consider packing it up and taking it with us. Of course, each book and file will need to be logged as evidence before it leaves this room." The rest of the team groaned at the prospect. "I'll give you a hand once I've tracked down Pauline and checked how she's getting on."

"That's a cop-out and you know it," Lorne grumbled.

"I'll need to see her if we've got to evidence this lot. We'll need to get some equipment from her before we can go ahead." Sally left the room again and went in search of the pathologist. "Pauline, are you around?"

A sudden breeze brushed past her as she entered the hallway, despite the front door being shut. Sally shuddered and said a silent prayer to keep her safe.

"You called?" Pauline appeared at the other end of the hallway. She walked towards Sally and asked, "Are you okay? You look like you've seen a ghost."

"You'll probably think I'm nuts but, I think I might have felt something brush past me."

Pauline stared at her, peered over her shoulder, and then faced Sally again. "I'm glad I'm not the only one who has felt something here."

Sally closed her eyes, an invisible hand clutching her heart. "Don't say that. I don't think I'll be able to stay here too long if I think it's haunted."

"Why not? It's probably all the tortured souls crying out for our help. I have no intention of letting them down, have you?"

"No, not at all."

"You wanted to see me?"

"Yes, to check how things are going with you."

"Did I see your senior officer here?"

"Yes, sorry, I'm an idiot. I should have introduced you to him. You probably wouldn't have met him yet."

"I haven't. Don't worry about it. Why was he here?"

"Not to check up on me, thankfully. He needed to see for himself the extent of the task we have on our hands."

"Will he sort out extra funding for us? Because we're going to need it."

"Yes, he's on his way back to the station now to have a word with the superintendent."

"Good. I also saw you talking to the divers. What news do you have from them?"

"That three sacks, possibly containing remains, have been discovered."

"I predict they will be the first of many."

"I think you're right. My team is busy sifting through the paperwork that was found in the secret office. They've found a journal listing boys' names, DOBs, and there's a letter beside each of the names, M or K."

"What?" Again, Pauline frowned.

"We suspect it means missing or killed."

"Oh, for fuck's sake, sorry, I should have made the connection myself. There's an awful lot for you to sift through in that room."

"Which is why I think we should transfer it back to the station. How do you want us to list it as evidence?"

"Do it when you get back. It makes sense for you to do it

in familiar surroundings. Maybe you can get extra hands to help you."

"Here's hoping. You're going to trust me to log it properly?"

Pauline stared at her and hitched up her shoulders. "Do we have an option? We're all up to our necks in it here."

"Okay, I'll get it organised then. Have you unearthed anything else down here yet?"

"Not yet. We're hoping that's it for now, but then we've got two more floors to go through. There are bound to be more horrors yet to uncover."

"I hope you're wrong, but I'm inclined to believe you're right. This investigation is already affecting me emotionally."

"Stop it. Don't go there. You can't let it get under your skin. All we can do is seek the truth and try to locate the families of the victims. Have you thought about running an appeal, yet?"

"I haven't. I wanted to see what evidence we found first."

Pauline tilted her head. "And now?"

"Yeah, I'll get the paperwork transferred back to the station with the rest of my team, and then seriously consider holding a press conference. It'll probably come as a genuine shock to the residents in this area."

"Maybe, maybe not. Perhaps they all had an inkling as to what was happening here and chose to ignore it. Or were forced to ignore it."

"Don't say that."

"Why not? You know as well as I do how some kids have been treated throughout history. I shouldn't have to remind you of that, Sally."

"I know. The chief and I had the same thought when we

came out of the 'torture room', that the equipment in there was used mainly for sexual gratification."

Pauline raised her upturned hands. "Like I said, kids have been constantly treated badly over the years. People have notoriously turned a blind eye to child abuse for decades, maybe even centuries."

Tears misted Sally's eyes at the thought. "Horrendous to believe there is that much wickedness in this world."

"It's a fact that is hard to dismiss, I'm afraid."

"Oh well, we're wasting time here discussing the ins and outs of what goes on in the minds of the depraved who allow these atrocities to happen. I'm sure you've got work to do. I'll call the station and get them to send us a van and some extra hands to get that lot shifted. You can trust us to document everything properly. I'll keep in touch. There's no point in me asking you how long you think you'll be here on site, is there?"

"How long is that piece of proverbial string again?"

Sally smiled, relieved that she and Pauline were back on speaking terms, with no sarcastic comments to fight off. "That long, eh? I don't envy you."

SEVERAL HOURS LATER, the team drove back to the station, where it took a human chain of officers to unload the van and carry the boxes of evidence they had uncovered in that room.

"What the hell?" Joanna shook her head and mumbled.

"I know. Don't ask. Our job will be to wade our way through that lot over the coming weeks."

"That will not be easy, boss."

"I agree, which is why I'm going to have a chat with the

chief about possibly adding to the team, if only temporarily. Otherwise, it'll be a daunting task for us."

Joanna nodded. "You're not wrong. I'd better get you all a coffee."

"Thanks. I'm sure everyone will appreciate it." Sally rested her backside on a nearby desk and asked, "Where the heck do we start?"

Lorne scratched her head and swept a few stray hairs behind her ear. "I suppose the ledgers we found. The ones with the kids' names."

Sally nodded. "Good call. You're right, of course. It's getting late. Let's give it our best shot for an hour, and then I suggest we call it a day and start afresh in the morning."

"Makes sense to me. I put the ledger away in one of the boxes and marked it on top. I just need to find that box."

"It's over there, Lorne." Jordan pointed at a box on its own on the other side of the room.

"Cheers, thanks, Jordan."

"I'll be right back," Sally said. She took off up the hallway to the chief's office.

"This is becoming a habit," Lyn said the second she laid eyes on her.

"Sorry. Hopefully, this will be the last time I have to pester him for a while. Has he told you what we found at the location?"

The secretary's mouth turned down at the side, and she shook her head. "He did. Hard to believe such atrocities went on there over the years."

"Did you know about the school when you were growing up?"

"I think I heard it mentioned by my parents once or twice. I can't for the life of me tell you what that entailed, though. Anyway, I'll let the chief know you're here. I'll be right back."

Sally paced the floor while she waited.

Lyn returned and nodded. "He'll see you now, Inspector. Can I get you a coffee?"

"You're very kind, but I have one waiting for me back at the office." Sally smiled and entered the chief's office.

"Ah, there you are. Back safe and sound. How's it going?"

Sally flopped into the chair opposite him. "Not too bad. We've brought back all the paperwork we found in that room. Would it be cheeky of me to ask for an extra pair of hands or two to help us sift through it all? The more hands we can get, the quicker Lorne and I can get on the road and start interviewing people."

"In other words, start piecing this intriguing puzzle together."

"Sums it up nicely, sir."

"Have a word with Pat on the front desk, see if he can spare anyone, bearing in mind we've already pinched a few of his men to conduct a search of the grounds out there."

"I know. Thanks, that's all I need for now."

"Glad to have been of service. Let me know how the investigation progresses. You know where I am if you need to run anything past me, okay?"

"I will. I promise. I'll leave you to get on with your boring paperwork." She grinned and walked out of the office.

"That was a quick one," Lyn said as Sally closed the door behind her.

"I've got a ton of work ahead of me. I'm eager to get down to business. Thanks, Lyn."

"Good luck, Inspector, it sounds like you're going to need it."

"You're not wrong."

Sally trotted back up the hallway to the main office, deciding it would be better to give the desk sergeant a call from there rather than asking him in person. The thought of going downstairs and back again eventually made her mind up for her. It had been a long day, and her body was reminding her of that with every move she made.

She picked up her coffee and went through to her office to make the call. "Hi, Pat. It's me again."

"Hello, Inspector, what do you need?"

"Can you spare someone to help us go through all the paperwork we brought back? Tomorrow will do."

"I'm sure I can find a willing volunteer for you. If you can leave it with me until the morning?"

"Brilliant. You're a star." She ended the call and drank half of her coffee, which was by now lukewarm, and cursed herself for not taking Lyn up on her offer to have a decent drink while she was there.

Lorne was bent over a box at the side of the room.

"Do you need a hand?" Sally asked.

"Christ, did you have to sneak up behind me like that? I thought you were in your office."

"Sorry. Pat's going to sort out an extra pair of hands for us in the morning. Hopefully, that will free up some spare time for us to get out and about."

"Sounds good. Don't forget, this lot will need to be listed as evidence, as well." Lorne sighed and puffed out her cheeks. "It's a mammoth task."

Sally lowered her voice and said, "I was thinking of tasking Joanna with that job. She's great at organising. It would be right up her street to do it."

"I was about to suggest the same."

"I'll have a word with her." Sally crossed the room and

tapped Joanna on the shoulder. The poor woman almost leapt out of her seat. "Oh, my Lord, I'm sorry. I didn't mean to creep up on you like that."

"I think we're all a little on edge with this investigation, boss. What can I do for you?"

"I think you're right. I've got a special job for you."

Joanna's eyes lit up. "You have?"

Sally smiled and said, "I wondered if you'd be up for logging all the evidence for us."

Joanna rubbed her hands together. "That would be an honour. I'd love to do it."

"I bet you won't be saying that in a couple of days."

They both laughed.

"Umm... how do you think I should do it? Box by box? I wouldn't want to hold the rest of the team up."

"Why don't we get the others to go through it a box at a time and then hand it over to you to list?"

"Sounds like a good plan to me. I'll get everything organised. The office is going to be in a mess for weeks."

"If not months," Sally agreed. She returned to give Lorne the good news and opened the journal Lorne had set on the desk beside her, ready to delve into.

"This is going to be one of the hardest investigations we've ever had to deal with during our careers, Sal."

"Emotionally and physically, and this is just the tip of the iceberg. We don't yet know what the other teams back at the house will unearth. I'm going to have to keep my eye on things out there, as well. If it were possible to split myself in two, now would be an ideal time to do it."

"I feel for you. You know we're all behind you every step of the way. The first thing we need to do is note down the names with the M beside them and check through the missing person files."

"I agree. Do you want me to make a start on that now, or first thing?"

"Will you have a quick look tonight? I'm eager to go home feeling we've achieved something today. At the moment, I can't say I'm thrilled by what we've accomplished so far."

Lorne stood upright and folded her arms. "What? Are you winding me up?"

Sally frowned. "You think differently?"

"Absolutely. I think we've gone above and beyond today. We showed up at Oakridge with nothing this morning and look around you. We've uncovered a goldmine that will hopefully lead us to at least make a few arrests."

"I wish I had your optimism, partner. Look at the dates in this book, and don't forget the letter I received. This shows that these incidents happened five decades ago, so even if the teachers were in their thirties back then, they would be in their eighties now. What's the likelihood of us finding the offenders alive?"

"These days, there is a higher probability of people living longer than there was twenty years ago. Don't be such a defeatist."

"I'm close to it. I'm trying to be a realist. Our situation might be tough right from the start."

Lorne shrugged. "No different to any other case we've worked on over the years. The one solid fact in our favour is what's surrounding us. All this paperwork to hand. How many cases have we been involved in that have given us this much information from the outset?"

Sally smiled. "You're right. I'm guilty of putting obstacles in the way right out of the starting gate; something a copper should never do."

"Exactly. If ever we needed to apply a positive mental attitude, it would be now; in this case."

"What we need to find is the personnel files. Listen up, guys. Before we leave tonight, I'd like to see if we can find either the personnel files for the staff during the time the school was operating, or a ledger with the names listed."

Stuart and Jordan gave a thumbs-up and continued to sift through the two boxes they were already searching.

Sally crossed her fingers and approached one of the untouched boxes.

"Do you want me to lend a hand?" Joanna asked.

"Everyone needs to chip in at this stage. Why don't you take this box here? Jordan, would you mind taking it over to Joanna's desk for me?"

"Sure thing, boss."

In just one hour, they achieved their goal and found the relevant personnel details to kick-start the investigation the next day.

"Okay, let's go home. It's been a long day. I'll see you all bright and early in the morning."

The team eagerly packed up the boxes they were working on, shut off their computers and left for the night.

Sally dropped Lorne off and headed home for the evening. Simon and Dex were playing fetch on the front lawn. "Hey, can I join in?"

"You can take over from me. I should be indoors, organising dinner. How did your day turn out in the end?"

"I'll tell you about it over dinner. I could do with stretching my legs down by the river, if that's all right with you?"

He inclined his head and said, "That bad, eh? I'll get a special bottle of wine out of the cellar to help cheer you up."

"Thanks. That's thoughtful of you. I need to switch coats.

I reckon it'll be chilly down by the river. What's on the menu for this evening?"

"Salmon, asparagus, broccoli, and I haven't decided yet what kind of potatoes to serve with it. Any preference?"

"What about a potato gratin? We haven't had one of those for ages."

He kissed the tip of her nose. "Gratin it is then. Enjoy your walk."

"I'm going to run upstairs and get changed first. I have the smell of death on me, even if I haven't, er... you know what I mean."

He laughed. "Bless you, I think so. Dex, inside for five minutes."

Dex ran into the house ahead of them. Sally went upstairs to the main bedroom but resisted the temptation to sit on the bed, fearing she might never get up again, feeling that tired. She had no doubts that a walk with her beloved pooch would put that right.

After changing into her jeans and a woolly jumper, she descended the stairs to find Dex waiting patiently, glancing up at his lead. "You're a good boy." She ruffled his head and attached the lead to his collar. "I won't be long," she shouted and left the house.

The wind had got up since she'd gone inside, and she zipped her coat up to keep it at bay. When they reached the banks of the river, she decided it wouldn't be right to let Dex off for a paddle, just in case he got swept away in the raging river. "Not today, boy. Let's have a stroll instead." She kept to the well-lit path for fifteen minutes, then turned to make her way back to the house.

Simon was serving up their meal when they arrived.

"Sorry, a neighbour stopped to have a chat," she said. "Penny's son has been in trouble with a gang of youths at the school. She wanted some advice. I told her I would send the community officer around to see her tomorrow."

"You never stop, do you?" He put the plates on the table and then turned his attention to the bottle of wine, which he had allowed to breathe for a while.

"This looks delicious."

He sat opposite her, beaming at the compliment. "Right, now you can tell me how your day panned out after we came to your rescue this morning."

"Christ, it seems an eternity ago that you left us at the house." Over dinner, ensuring that her meal didn't go cold in the process, she told him what the teams had discovered.

"Bloody hell. Sounds like SOCO and Pauline are going to be on site for a few weeks to come."

"Yeah, I thought the same. I don't think she's looking forward to that one iota. It was nothing short of horrific in there. One of those instances where Lorne and I couldn't wait to make our escape."

"How awful. Mind you, from a pathologist's point of view, I would have found it an intriguing case to work on. Of course, there would be added pressure to ensure everything was documented thoroughly and every nook and cranny was searched to within an inch of its life, but what an honour to be involved with what could turn out to be the investigation of the century."

"I never thought of that. I don't think Pauline was too enamoured when she first arrived. However, by the time we left, her mood had mellowed. Yes, let's put it that way."

"From what you've told me about her... no, let's not go there." He laughed.

"Yeah, I think you're right. She's a strange one to work out most of the time. But on the plus side, I've never felt the need to question her work or the results she's supplied us with."

"Then that's all that matters. Top-up?"

"I thought you'd never ask. Another one of your special wines which has gone to waste."

"Gone to waste? I wouldn't say that. Yes, I could have left it for a special occasion, but it's put a smile on our faces. That should be a justification in itself to raid the cellar."

"I'm not complaining."

"So, how long do you foresee the teams being out there?"

"Weeks, who knows? That might stretch into months yet. There are three floors to search."

He shook his head. "Let's hope she's up for the challenge."

"Me, too."

4

Lorne rang her the following morning at seven and asked if she fancied starting early. Sally agreed and scheduled to pick up her partner at eight-fifteen, giving them both time to shower and have breakfast.

When they arrived at the station, Sally was pleased to see the rest of the team had the same idea. "You guys are the best. I don't tell you that often enough. I appreciate your work ethic and eagerness to get on with the investigation. Let's try to hit the ground running today."

Lorne supplied everyone with a coffee, and Sally took hers to the office to sift through the pile of paperwork that had landed on her desk overnight. Before she tackled it, she sat down and checked in with Pauline.

"Hello, is that you, Sally?"

"It is. I was wondering how you were getting on."

Pauline groaned. "We're back at it. The team and I have been at the location since eight. Nothing further to report so far from our end, but the divers found yet another body in the lake."

"Shit! Not what I wanted to hear. Bugger, okay. My team is hard at it, too. We're going through all the paperwork. Lorne and I are hoping to get the investigation in full swing before the morning is out. Thanks for sparing the time to speak with me, and Simon sends his regards. Said to pass on his best wishes for dealing with the case."

"No chance of him coming out of retirement for a few weeks to lend us a hand, is there?"

Sally chuckled. "I know what the answer would be without running it past him. A categorical no."

"Yeah, I suspected that might be the answer. It was worth a try," Pauline replied, sounding as if she was dreading what the day had in store for her and her team. "I must plough on. Have a good day."

"Ditto. I'll be in touch if we find anything."

"Me, too."

Sally ended the call and tackled her paperwork for the next thirty minutes. What she hadn't dealt with in that time, she put back in her in-tray, aware that she would have DCI Green's full backing, considering what needed to be done towards the new investigation.

She rejoined the team and asked Lorne what she had found.

"Joanna found out who the owner was, Norris Hermon. He died in 1975 at seventy. He had no family so died intestate. The school continued to be in business for five years but closed after funds ran out. The government claimed it and held on to it for a few years, then passed it over to the local council. Because it had deteriorated so badly, it was just left."

"What a shame. It's a beautiful building, but I agree, the cost would have been exorbitant to bring it back to its former glory." Sally shuddered at the thought of someone purchasing the property and spending millions on it, only to find it haunted by the tortured souls of the boys who had been killed there. "Did anyone sense anything while you were there?"

The rest of the team looked at her blankly.

Then Lorne asked, "Don't tell me you did?"

"Just to clarify, Pauline felt something there, as well, so it's not just me."

Lorne shrugged. "Hey, you know I'm a believer. Fuck..."

"What's wrong? The colour has drained from your face."

"Carol."

"Carol who?" Sally gasped. "No. God, yes. Would she?"

Lorne chewed on her lip. "I could ask her. What do you think?"

"It's got to be worth a shot. Despite us finding this lot, I can't see it answering all our questions, can you?"

"I agree. Shall I call her?"

"That would be cool. No pressure from me, though, if she's not up to it." Sally's heart raced at the prospect of having the exceptional Carol working alongside them again. She'd had the pleasure of dealing with the psychic several times over the years and been amazed at her perception. Of course, Lorne had worked with her many times during her spell serving in the Met, with much success. "Go into my office to make the call."

Lorne didn't need to ask twice. She dashed in there but left the door ajar. Sally followed her and put her finger to her lips to stop the others either talking or laughing at her antics as she earwigged Lorne's conversation. She tiptoed back to where Lorne was sitting when she overheard her partner say goodbye to Carol.

"How did you get on?"

"She jumped at the chance of helping us out and told me she'd been expecting my call."

Sally thumped her thigh. "Wow, really? Why didn't we think about asking her sooner?"

"I just didn't think about it. It wasn't until you mentioned you thought you'd felt something there that it dawned on me to ask her."

"When is she arriving? Do we need to pick her up?"

"No, she's going to check on the train times. Carol will be here by the end of the day. She'll stay with me, so we won't have a hotel bill to cover."

"I can sort something out for you through petty cash."

Lorne waved away the suggestion. "It'll be fun having her stay with us. Don't worry about it."

"I'm intrigued to know what she said when you raised the subject."

"I got the impression she was on the verge of tears. She said that she could visualise the torture some of the children went through."

"This is going to be so harrowing to listen to, isn't it?"

"Judging by experience, that's an understatement. I hate to say this, but do you think you should have run the idea past the chief first?"

Sally sighed and rolled her eyes. "Shit. You're right. Okay, I'll go and see him now. One last question before I go."

"What's that?" Lorne asked.

"Do you think Carol will tell us who wrote the letter?"

"Maybe, we'll have to wait and see. Wouldn't it be marvellous if she could?"

"Never say never." Sally cringed and crossed the room to the main door. "I'll be right back. I can't say I'm looking forward to running the idea past him."

"You'll be fine. Just enforce upon him what an asset she will be, working alongside us. We need to ensure he doesn't think we'll depend completely on what she tells us."

"I'll do that." During her trek to DCI Green's office, Sally repeatedly rehearsed what she wanted to say.

Lyn glanced up from her computer and stopped typing. "Inspector? This is becoming a daily occurrence."

"Sorry. I could do with seeing him. It's pretty urgent. How is he fixed?"

Lyn checked the phone to confirm that none of the lights were illuminated. "He should be free. Let me poke my head in and ask for you."

"Thanks, Lyn."

The secretary left her desk and knocked on the chief's door. "Sorry to disturb you, sir. DI Parker would like a quick word with you if you can spare her a minute or two."

"Again? Okay, very well. Send her in."

Lyn gave Sally the thumbs-up, and she inhaled a large breath and released it as she walked towards Green's office.

"Sorry to interrupt you, sir. I won't keep you long."

"Come in and take a seat. How is it going over at Oakridge Hall?"

"Since you were there, another body has been found in the lake."

He tutted and shook his head. "That's sad news. Are the divers still searching?"

"I believe so, yes."

"Thank you for the update."

Sally scratched the back of her neck and faltered to find the right words to begin. *So much for practising on my way here.*

"Is there something else, Inspector?"

"I feel it is my duty... umm... I think it's only right for me... umm..."

"Spit it out, woman. What's going on in that head of yours? I know when you're hatching some kind of plan. What is it?"

"You're probably not going to like this, but given the intricacies of the case, shall we say, Lorne has been in touch with her psychic friend."

He raised both of his hands. "Now wait just a second."

"But, sir, please. She's worked with us before."

He ran his hands through his hair and then placed them on the top of his head. "Oh, no. Don't ask me to do this. I'll never live it down."

Sally smiled. "Is that all you're worried about? Your reputation?"

"Aren't you? If the press gets hold of this, they'll tear you apart."

"I'm willing to take the risk. Especially if she can deliver some crucial answers for us."

He narrowed his eyes at her and asked, "There's something else you're not telling me, isn't there?"

"There is, but I'd rather not say in case you question my sanity."

"Oh, hell. You're going to have to tell me now. Come on, you can speak freely in this office. You know that, Sally. There will be no judgement on my part."

Sally hesitated briefly until he gestured for her to get on with it. "I'm only telling you this to give you an idea as to why I asked Lorne to get in touch with Carol."

He smiled and relaxed in his chair. "You've seen something out there, haven't you?"

Sally's gaze dropped to his desk. Suddenly feeling foolish, she struggled to maintain eye contact with him. "Please don't mock me, sir."

"I'm not. Have you?"

"I felt something brush past me, and before you laugh, I discussed the matter with the pathologist, and she told me she'd felt a presence there, too."

"She has? Well, if she's prepared to back up your theory about the place being haunted, then I have to believe you, don't I?"

"I didn't mention it to the rest of the team until this morning. That's when Lorne reminded me about her psychic friend. I know I should have run the idea past you first, but I just thought we'd need all the help we can get on this investigation. We've been at it for days now, and to say we're underwhelmed by what we've got so far, delving through the archives, would be an understatement."

"So you rang Carol? And what did she have to say?"

"Lorne did. She didn't have to say much because Carol had been expecting Lorne's call."

He sprang forward in his chair once more. "What? Are you telling me that some of these spirits have already contacted her?"

"So it would seem. She's agreed to lend a hand and is arriving later. I'm not sure at what time. I'm guessing she'll want to make a start in the morning. That is, if you have got no objections to her coming aboard, sir."

"Looks like the decision has been taken out of my hands, doesn't it?"

"Not necessarily. If you tell me to send her packing, I will."

"No, I won't tell you to do that. If you believe she is the missing link to help you solve this investigation, then far be it for me to either question your judgement or stand in your way."

Sally let out a sigh, and the tightness in her shoulders evaporated. "God, I'm so relieved to hear you say that, sir. Here I was, thinking I'd made a mistake telling you what our plans comprise, and that you'd think I had lost my mind."

He grinned. "Like me, you probably lost that years ago, when we first signed up to be coppers, right?"

Sally chuckled. "You're not wrong. At least, it feels like that most days."

"Now go, let me get on with some important work that awaits my attention."

"Oops, I'm sorry to have disturbed you, sir."

"No, you're not and you're forgiven. If anything, I welcomed the distraction, even if the proposal was a slightly bizarre one."

Sally left her seat and smiled at him. "Thanks for understanding and for giving me your backing."

"One question before you leave, if I may?"

She dropped back into her seat again. "What's that?"

"Have you considered holding a press conference yet?"

"I'd like to hold off going down that route for now, if it's all the same to you, sir."

"Because of Carol's reputation?"

"Yes, she's that good I doubt if we'll need any help from the general public, although I'm still keen to speak with the author of the letter I received."

"It'll be interesting to see if they come forward. I wonder if they're monitoring the proceedings out at Oakridge."

That suggestion hadn't even crossed her mind before now. "Damn, I never even thought about that. I'll make sure I survey the area the next time I'm out there."

"That'll be imminent, surely? Visiting the site is crucial for Carol to get a genuine sense of what we're up against."

"I suppose so. We'll know more tomorrow. I can't quite describe it, but I'm feeling a new-found confidence in cracking this investigation that has evaded me until now."

"I can understand where you're coming from. I have one word of advice for you, Inspector. Never doubt your abilities. You're better than you think you are. Which is why I'm prepared to leave you alone and allow you to get on with your work without me interfering most of the time."

"Thank you for that, sir. I appreciate your faith in me and my team."

"Always. Now let me get back to the mindless stuff, which keeps me tied to my desk most days."

"I'm going this time, I promise. I am grateful for your understanding of the situation and your unwavering belief in my abilities, sir."

"Make sure my reputation isn't put in jeopardy over this investigation."

"I'll do my best." She rose from her seat and walked towards the door.

"I have every confidence that you won't let me down."

"No pressure then." Sally smiled and left the office. She leaned against the wall and exhaled a breath.

"That bad, eh?"

"Worse," Sally replied. "I'm just hoping that my request doesn't come back and bite me in the arse."

"I'm confident that won't happen. He admires you as an officer and is grateful to have someone with your abilities on his team."

"Wow, thanks, Lyn. I wouldn't have guessed, not by my experience. Although, he appears to have mellowed lately. Dare I say it, since his separation from his wife?"

"They're divorced now."

"Blimey, that was quick."

"And yes, I agree with you. He's much more pleasant to deal with these days. That sounded disrespectful. I didn't mean he was an ogre in the past."

Sally grinned. "It's fine. I knew exactly what you meant. Well, I'd better get on with my day."

"How is the investigation going? Or shouldn't I ask?"

Sally held her hand out in front of her and waved it from side to side. "Can you ask me that question again in a couple of days?"

"Sorry to hear it. I should imagine cold cases are the worst type to solve."

"Some cases are harder to break than others. I think you can say this one is one of the worst my team and I have encountered over the years. Hopefully, that's about to change for the better."

"Oh? Care to share what you have planned?"

Sally winked and said, "If I told you, I'd have to kill you. Enjoy the rest of your day, Lyn."

"Oh my. I wish I hadn't asked now," Lyn said, clearly put out by Sally's retort.

"Sorry, I was joking, of course. Sometimes I have a wicked sense of humour."

"I've heard. Good luck, Inspector."

Sally's steps were lighter on the way back, and when she walked through the door to the main office, her entire team glanced her way. A sea of worried expressions awaiting news about how her meeting had gone. "He's fine about us having Carol on board during the investigation."

Lorne swept a hand over her face. "Thank goodness for that. The longer you were gone, the more anxious we were becoming."

Sally walked towards the drinks station, but Joanna stopped her.

"I'll fix you a drink, boss. We've just had one."

"Thanks." Sally joined Lorne and sat at the empty desk opposite her. "I can't believe he accepted it without throwing a wobbly."

"Wow, neither can I. Maybe inviting him to that barbecue a few months back has made him mellow towards you," Lorne suggested.

Sally leaned in and whispered, "I think it's more likely to do with the fact that he's divorced now."

"Oh, I knew it was on the cards. I didn't realise it had gone through yet. We all know the toll that going through a divorce can take on you. We've both been there."

"Yep. No, he was in good spirits. Excuse the pun."

Lorne laughed. "You are funny. Seriously, I'm glad he didn't kibosh the plan. There's nothing worse than dealing with a senior officer who is a sceptic. I found myself in a perpetual battle with Sean Roberts over that aspect."

"How did you handle it?"

"I ignored him and kept him out of the loop. Only informed him that I'd used Carol's services at the end of an investigation instead of halfway through. He used to be furious and never heaped praise on her abilities."

"He was a prat, though, wasn't he?"

"Yep." Lorne shuddered. "And to think I dated him before I got involved with Tom."

Sally screwed her nose up. "The things we do when we're young and innocent have a habit of coming back to haunt us. Ouch, excuse the pun again."

They both laughed. Joanna arrived with her coffee.

"Thanks, Joanna. Right, let's get our day started."

"Speak for yourself. Some of us have been at it an hour or more."

Sally flashed her a toothy grin. "I expect you to have some news for me then."

"Dream on. No, I think I've found something we can get our teeth stuck into."

Intrigued, Sally sat forward. "Tell me more."

"We've got the personnel files in the form of a ledger. To my reckoning, for the size of the building, I don't think there are enough teachers listed here." Lorne handed Sally a heavy book. In it were three names.

"Are you kidding me? Three names? There had to be more teachers on site than this... unless these were the men who were torturing, or brutalising, the children. Maybe they were part of a special group."

"That's the conclusion I came to. Also, Stuart has stumbled across something that could prove significant."

Sally swivelled in her chair and asked, "What's that, Stu?"

"I found a journal with a list of names and an amount beside each of them."

Sally's eyes widened, and a sickening sensation trickled down the length of her spine. "No, tell me they didn't sell the kids?"

Stuart shook his head. "I don't think in that sense, boss. The amount listed wouldn't be enough to buy a child, even when we factor inflation into the equation."

"I don't get it. What are you saying then? Oh shit, no, sorry, I think I'm with you now. You think the kids were prostituted?"

Stuart nodded. His expression was a mixture of sadness and anger. "There's more, boss."

Sally closed her eyes, dreading what he was about to tell her. "Go on, hit me with it."

"We've researched the names and, back in the day, they were all local dignitaries."

"Tell her," Lorne ordered.

Sally's gaze darted between Lorne and Stuart. "Yes, I need to hear the full facts, Stu."

"Some of these people were serving police officers."

"What the fuck? Shit, if this gets out... Holy shit! What ranks are we talking about?"

"Some as high up as Chief Superintendent."

Sally put her mug on the desk and then covered her face with her hands. "No, no, no."

"Adding to the flames," Lorne said, "it might explain why we haven't been able to find anything in the archives."

"And would also explain why all this was buried behind a secret wall. Fuck, we're going to need to tread carefully going forward. Who was running this establishment? The owner? What was his name again? Norris something or other."

"Norris Hermon. Neither of us has found any proof that he was anything other than the owner or backer of the facility. Whether he knew what was going on there, we'll never know because he died back in the seventies."

Sally shook her head in disbelief. "Jesus, this is going way beyond what I thought we'd find when we started to search Oakridge. It's concerning me where this is going to lead."

"That shouldn't stop us digging, though," Lorne said.

"I totally agree. I'm mindful of the impact this information might have on Carol."

"Don't worry. I'll have a word with her and prepare her for what lies ahead. However, she gave me the impression that she already knows. Which is why she was eager to offer her services. The last I heard, she was winding down and considering retirement."

"I hope it's not going to affect her too much."

"She would have taken a step back if she didn't want to help us. The question is, what do we do about the names in that ledger?"

"Christ, these people, I'm presuming they're all men, are they?"

Stuart nodded.

"Have you checked if they're still alive?" Sally asked.

"Some are. The other bastards are all dead. Sorry, boss, I shouldn't have been so disrespectful."

"You said what we're all thinking, Stuart. Just a warning to all of you. Until we know what we're dealing with, any information we stumble across remains in this room. I know it'll be a tough task and that we're already affected by what we've learnt about Oakridge, but we must set aside our personal opinions regarding the historical events which have blighted that establishment. Okay?"

The team either nodded or raised a thumb in her direction.

"Thanks, folks." She faced Lorne again and asked, "Damn, do you think I should seek Green's advice on this one, or should we see what comes of it first?"

"It's a tough one. If it were down to me, I would see what unfolds first. If these individuals are proven to have committed these heinous crimes, I believe they should face justice, regardless of their positions."

Sally's heart rate escalated at the prospect. She knew Lorne was right but, when it came to the crunch, it would be her neck on the chopping block, no one else's. "Maybe I should just have a quick word. Tell him what we've found, while he's in a good mood."

Lorne shrugged. "All it will do is show him you're lacking in confidence. He trusts you to do the right thing, Sal."

Sally gulped down the saliva filling her mouth. "I'm torn. It's a no-win situation."

"It is. But your priority must remain with the victims, that's our job. We shouldn't be worried about whose toes we're likely to tread on in the process."

"I know you're right and, former colleagues or not, they deserve to have the book thrown at them."

"I agree, the reason we became police officers in the first place was because we wanted to see justice served. They're the ones in the wrong, not you, not us. They used those kids for what we assume was their own sexual gratification. The kids, from what we have learnt so far, were between the ages of eight and ten. That's sickening." The rest of the team applauded Lorne's speech. "There's no need for that, guys. I'm only speaking the truth."

"Okay, you've convinced me. Let's see what we can dig up on the men who are still with us, and Lorne and I will visit them."

Lorne raised her eyebrows. "That could prove interesting."

"Can you get the list of teachers together and find out where they live? And we can kill two birds with one stone."

"Sure. I'll get on it now." Lorne's phone tinkled, and she read the text message. "It's from Carol. Her train is due to arrive in Norwich at four this afternoon. All right if I ring Tony to see if he can pick her up?"

"Go for it. If he's too busy, we'll drop by and do it instead."

"We can't do that. We'll have too much to do."

Sally winked at her. "Where there's a will, there's a way."

Lorne trotted into Sally's office and returned a few moments later. "All sorted. Tony was happy to do it, and Simon agreed. All I need to do now is text Carol back. She'll be fretting, wondering if I've received her message or not."

"The older generation, eh? My dad is the same. Is Tony looking forward to having your guest stay for a few days?"

"He's fine. They get on well together." Lorne tapped on her phone, and Carol's response came straight back. "See, I told you."

They laughed.

"Back to work. I'm delighted Carol will be joining us. Let's see if we can get the ball rolling today, to ease the pressure on her when she turns up. Why don't we start by visiting the teachers? Joanna, while we're out, if we give you the list of boys, can you do the necessary searches for us on the missing persons' register?"

"Fine by me." Lorne handed the relevant ledger over to Joanna and returned to tuck her chair under her desk.

"And Stuart and Jordan, if you can keep going through, damn, what shall we call it? Hmm… the 'visitors' book'. Yes, let's go with that. Note down any names and addresses of interest; obviously, we're only concerned about the men who are still with us today."

"On it now, boss," Stuart replied.

An hour later, Sally and Lorne headed out for a few hours to question the three members of the staff they had tracked down.

"Let's hope we find them in good health," Sally muttered, more out of hope than expectation.

"Fingers crossed. Although the likelihood of that being

true is probably zilch, given their ages range between eighty-four and eighty-seven."

Sally drew up outside a detached house in what appeared to be a pleasant neighbourhood on an old estate in Mattishall. "I haven't been out here in a while. I hope he's up to seeing us. He's the only one not in a care home."

They exited the car, and Sally inhaled and exhaled several times as they walked up the short path to the front door. Sally rang the bell, and they waited patiently for it to be answered. She was about to ring it a second time when a man in his eighties opened it.

He frowned and looked both of them up and down.

Sally noticed he had a cane supporting him. She showed him her warrant card. "Mr Rowe? I'm DI Sally Parker, and this is my partner, DS Lorne Warner. Is it possible for us to come in and have a brief chat with you, sir?"

His gaze drifted between them, and Sally could sense the cogs turning in his mind.

"About what?"

Sally held her hand up, and raindrops splattered her palm. "It's raining. If you don't mind, inside would be better."

"It's not convenient. I'm about to give my wife her lunch."

"I promise we won't keep you too long, sir."

He huffed out a breath and mumbled something incomprehensible. They followed him into the house.

He pointed at their feet. "Take your shoes off, especially if it's wet out there."

They slipped their shoes off and left them on the welcome mat, not that they'd received much of a welcome. Sally could tell they were going to have a battle on their hands.

"You'd better come through to the kitchen. I don't like to leave my wife, Ellen, alone for long."

He led the way into a kitchen that dated back to the nineteen nineties and required modernisation, judging by the way some doors were out of line and hanging at an angle. The trim was also missing from the worktops in several areas, too. "I'd offer you a seat, but there's not much room around the table once I put Ellen's wheelchair in place."

His wife offered them a weak smile. She seemed frail, her hands twisted with arthritis. Sally's heart went out to her.

Mr Rowe wheeled his wife into position at the table and collected a sandwich he'd made and a cup and saucer from the worktop on his left. "It's all right, love. These ladies are from the police."

"Oh no. Why? What have you been up to?"

He smiled and patted her left hand affectionately. "I can't think, love. I never go out, not without you by my side. Maybe they're here to issue us with a speeding ticket. I suppose we whizzed around the park the other day, trying to beat the rain, didn't we?"

His wife giggled. "Yes, that was a fun outing, until the rain came. Can I still eat my lunch?"

"Yes, we won't let them interfere with that, love. You're hungry, aren't you?" He glanced up at Sally and said, "It's important for us to stick to a routine, isn't it?"

"Yes. My tummy has been rumbling for at least an hour."

He pulled out a chair next to his wife and fed her the sandwich. She took the smallest nibble and chewed it half a dozen times before she opened her mouth to accept another bite.

Sally and Lorne remained standing and rested against

the worktop. Lorne withdrew her notebook from her coat pocket.

Sally cleared her throat and said, "We apologise for showing up out of the blue today."

"Why are you here?" Mr Rowe said, his eyes narrowed as he concentrated on the task at hand; feeding his wife. After another mouthful, she refused to eat anything else. "Come on, Ellen, you've barely touched your food."

"I'm full. I've had enough. Can I have my tea in the lounge? I'm cold. I want to sit in front of the fire."

He smiled at his wife and shrugged at Sally. "Ellen's needs must come first. I'll get her settled in front of the TV, and then we can have a chat."

"Of course. We're in no rush."

Using a serviette, he wiped his wife's mouth and then guided her to the hallway. He returned moments later to collect the cup and saucer and gave them an embarrassed smile. "I won't be long. You watch the TV. You like that programme, don't you?"

"I do. Thank you, Howard. I suppose a piece of cake is out of the question."

"I'll cut you a slice once I've spoken to the officers, all right?"

"If you insist."

The sound on the TV went up, and seconds later, Howard appeared in the doorway to the kitchen. "I'm sorry to keep you."

"Caring for your wife must keep you busy," Sally said.

"You have no idea. I don't have a life of my own. I've been Ellen's carer for the last ten years. I'm the only one she hasn't pissed off or struck out at in that time."

"Sorry to hear that. Do you have any family members who can help?"

"Nope. They're too busy with their own lives to even consider giving me any respite. They haven't got a clue what I have to contend with day in and day out. As long as they're happy enough in their own little worlds, that's all that matters to them."

"That's unforgivable. You have my sympathy."

He shook his head and glared at her. "I don't need anyone's sympathy. I love my wife and will do everything I can to ensure she's safe and happy."

"That's admirable of you. May I ask why you use a cane?"

"I'm eighty-four. My legs aren't what they used to be."

"How do you care for your wife if you're suffering, as well?"

"We just do. I refuse to put her in a home. She's loved here, I do my very best for her. If I put her in a home, and I don't mean this disrespectfully, she wouldn't have the one-to-one care she receives here."

"I suppose that's true. May I ask what's wrong with her?"

"She was diagnosed with MS around ten years ago. The doctors are amazed by how long she has lived. Every doctor or consultant we've seen in that time has praised me for caring for her so well."

Sally smiled. Under different conditions, she believed she would have had a good connection with the man. "It must be a difficult situation to deal with."

"It's not easy, and it would be nice to have a break now and again, but as long as there are people like me who are willing to care for their spouses, the worthless government doesn't give a shit. Most of the homes in this area are full to bursting, so even a few days or hours of respite care is out of the question. I imagine you're not here because of our difficult predicament."

"No, that's right." Sally interlocked her fingers and clenched her hands. "We believe you were a teacher at Oakridge Hall. Is that correct?"

His eyes widened, and he gulped. "You know for a fact I was. Why?"

"For how long?"

"Long enough. Why?" he repeated. A twitch developed in his right eye, and he rubbed at it.

Sally noticed his hands were shaking. She was eager to get to the truth but conscious that the man's ill health might work against them. Treading carefully, she asked, "How was your time at the school?"

"What sort of question is that?"

"A genuine one. Did you enjoy working there?"

He stared at her and frowned. "I get the impression that you're trying to trip me up, Inspector. If you have something to say, I'd rather you didn't beat about the bush. Just come out and say what's on your mind, because this interview could be over in a few minutes if Ellen cries out for me. She remains my utmost priority, regardless of your opinion."

"Okay, I'll get to the point. A few days ago, I received an anonymous letter in the post from a concerned member of the public. Specific undisclosed details were highlighted in the letter for the first time. Are you aware of anything bad happening at the school during your time there?"

"Not really. Such as?"

"At this stage, I can't go into detail. Currently, the pathology team and SOCO are at Oakridge Hall, and what they've discovered is truly shocking."

His gaze dropped to the table. He wrung his hands together until his knuckles turned white, but he didn't respond.

"Nothing to say for yourself?"

"I'm thinking."

"About the atrocities that were carried out during your time at the school? Were you involved in them?"

He closed his eyes and exhaled a deep breath. "I don't want this to affect my life. Me caring for my wife. She can't live without me. Please, have mercy on me."

Raising an eyebrow, Sally lowered her voice and said, "Answer me this, did you show the boys at the school any mercy?"

He covered his eyes with a shaking hand. "Please, I'm begging you, don't do this. Not to Ellen. Can't you set this aside for a few years until she's no longer with us?"

"What? I find that request incredulous. How dare you?"

He dropped his hand and snarled at her, "It's been fifty fucking years!"

"And? You believe because these crimes happened half a century ago that you and the others involved in these deplorable crimes should remain free? We found dead bodies buried behind walls and possibly more dead bodies at the bottom of the lake. The families of those children deserve justice, wouldn't you agree?"

"Oh shit! I'm sorry for what happened to the boys, but it's been fifty years."

Sally sat back and glared at him. "And you and your colleagues thought you'd got away with it?"

"No, not at all. Life moves on. Five decades ago! Can't we just forget those times ever happened?"

Sally faced Lorne and shook her head. "I can't believe what I'm hearing, can you, Sergeant?"

"No, it's deplorable for Mr Rowe to ask us to ignore what we've discovered over the past few days."

"I agree with you," Sally said. "You're going to need to

come with us. We'll interview you under caution back at the station."

He pushed his chair back and winced. "Ouch, I can't. Neither my wife nor I are up to this right now."

"Unfortunately, that is not our problem. If we believe a serious crime or several crimes have been committed, we're quite within our rights to interview you immediately."

"Have you not listened to a bloody word I've said about our situation? I can't leave her. No, I refuse to leave her. I don't want her going to a home. That'll kill her."

Sally sighed. "Don't try to turn the tables on us, make us out to be the bad guys here. I believe you and your colleagues murdered innocent children. The victims and their families deserve justice, whether those vile acts took place last week or fifty years ago. Answer me this, if you would. How have you lived with yourself for five decades, knowing what lies behind the walls of that former school?"

His hand covered his eyes again, and his shoulders jiggled as the tears welled up.

Sally rolled her eyes at Lorne, who returned the gesture.

"I didn't mean to get involved. It was expected of us. Most of the kids that came to us didn't have families."

"What? And that gave you the green light to kill them? Because you thought they wouldn't be missed?"

He nodded, and Sally's heart flipped. At least, that's what it felt like.

"That's disgusting," she said. "Who was in charge at the time?"

He sat upright and pulled a tissue from the box on the table. "Mr Gorman. Frank Gorman was the headmaster. It was when he arrived that things changed."

"In what way?"

"Until then, there had been little to no discipline at the

school. Within a month of him taking up his post, he'd turned everything on its head."

"What does that mean?" Sally asked, intrigued.

"It means that he split the boys up into different classes." He paused to take a breath. "The boys who had come to the school because there was no one else to take them in were separated from the boys who went home to their families every night."

"You're telling me it wasn't a proper boarding school?"

"No, it used to be half and half."

"And the bodies we've found are the boys who had no living relatives. Is that what you're saying?" *That will explain why we've got nowhere with the missing person database. Those fuckers thought they were within their rights to rob these poor children of their lives because no one would know they were missing. Bastards! Keep calm. I need to get more information out of him yet.*

He nodded. His mouth twisted as if he were chewing the inside of his cheek. "I couldn't speak out against what was happening."

Sally raised an eyebrow and asked, "Do you mind telling me why?"

"Because I needed the job. Gorman had us by the short and curlies. I had been in trouble with the police, in and out of prison, for years. I started training to be a teacher whilst I was inside. The government was crying out for them around that time. Their suggestion was to reform prisoners who had 'lesser records', if that makes sense. I met Ellen when she came to visit a relative. I was keen to change my life for the better and agreed to go on the fast-track teaching course they were offering."

"Jesus, are you telling me the truth? The government handed the kids to you on a plate?"

"There weren't the stringent checks back then as there are today."

"Is that an excuse for what you did?"

"No. I didn't say that. I'm trying to tell you that there was a shortage, and this was the answer the government ultimately came up with."

"Did the government tell you to kill the boys?" As soon as the question left her lips, something scary dawned on her. *The dignitaries! This was their way in. Disgusting shits.*

"You can't ask me that."

"I think you'll find I can, and I just did."

He fidgeted in his seat and swept a hand through his short grey hair. "Not in so many words, no."

"Sorry, I don't understand."

He violently shook his head. "No, no more. I'm not prepared to say anything else without a solicitor being present. I know my rights."

"Hmm... I'm sure you do. Very well. We're going to have to take you in for questioning."

"I refuse to go with you. I've already explained that I can't leave Ellen on her own. Please, give me the rest of the day to make the arrangements. You have my word that I'll show up."

"Against my better judgement, I will relent and give you twenty-four hours to report to the station. I'm warning you, if you don't show up, a warrant for your arrest will be issued."

"I swear. My wife comes first."

"Give me your phone number, just in case."

"Trust me. I'm too bloody old to go on the run, Inspector. I'm sure, as this is an emergency, my daughter will come and stay with her mother for a few days."

"That's good news. Do you want to call her now while we're here?"

"Not really."

"It wasn't a question. I was advising you to ring your daughter. We will not leave until you can assure us that you'll show up at the station tomorrow."

"I see. Okay, let me get my phone. It's in the lounge."

He left the room.

Sally leaned in to whisper, "Do you trust him?"

"Nope, not in the slightest. The one positive in our favour is that we know where to find him if he lets us down."

Sally smiled as he returned to the kitchen. "Any good?"

"Yes. Tracie said she's willing to come over tomorrow to spend the night if it's needed."

"Excellent news. Did you tell her why?"

"I made up an excuse. I told her I had to stay overnight in hospital for a minor procedure."

"Even after all these years, you're still lying to your family."

He had the decency to look ashamed, and his gaze dropped to his feet. "Please don't think badly of me, Inspector, not until you have all the facts to hand."

"Ah, but here I am, giving you twenty-four hours to rehearse your story."

His gaze met hers. "That's unfair. I promise to tell you the truth. What have I got to lose this late in the day?"

She grinned and said two words, "Your freedom."

The colour drained from his ruddy cheeks. "You wouldn't? Not after all these years?"

"We tend to punish murderers in this country, no matter what age they are or how long ago the crime occurred."

He mumbled an expletive and sank into the chair he'd

recently vacated. "I never thought it would come to this. I wasn't the only one, you know."

"We're aware of that. Don't say anything else until you have your solicitor by your side."

He sprang out of his chair and winced, suddenly forgetting he had a bad leg. "It's not fair if you just come after me."

"You didn't listen to what I said. I told you we know that other men were involved. My advice would be to ring your solicitor after you've calmed down."

"And what if he's not available?"

"Then we can arrange a duty solicitor to join you. Either way, we will interview you tomorrow."

"You're a hard woman, Inspector."

"You think? I'm not the one who has taken the lives of several children and hidden their bodies for fifty years. So, you might want to reconsider your assumption of me." Sally rose from her seat and glanced at her watch. "Be at the station no later than eleven tomorrow morning, or I'll obtain a warrant for your arrest."

"So you've already said. There's nothing wrong with my memory or my hearing."

She walked into the hallway. "I'll remind you of that during the interview tomorrow, should you start flinging those types of excuses our way."

"I won't."

"Howard, are you finished with the police officers now?"

"Yes, dear. I'm showing them out now."

"Good. I'm lonely. I could do with some company."

He turned sideways at the door; Sally sensed he was struggling to hold back the tears. Guilt playing its part with his emotions.

Sally and Lorne slipped on their shoes and left the house.

"We'll see you tomorrow, Mr Rowe."

"I'll be there." He slammed the door behind them.

"Ouch, he wasn't too happy come the end," Sally said.

"Nope, I think the guilt set in, as well."

"I'm not surprised. It's probably just occurred to him he'll never get out of prison or see his wife again."

"That's tough. The poor woman will be devastated when she learns the truth."

"Yep, I'll feel sorry for his wife and family when the shit hits the fan. On to the next one. Both men are in a care home, aren't they? Is it the same one?"

"I believe so." Lorne flicked through her notebook. "Yes. The Lawns Care Home in Cringleford."

"I hope we don't come up against a brick wall with the manager of the home."

"There's every chance that might happen."

5

The care home was at the end of a cul-de-sac. Neither of them had been there before. They entered the building and approached the receptionist on duty.

Sally flashed her ID. "Is it possible to speak with the manager, please?"

"Miss Short is dealing with a patient at the moment. Would you like to take a seat? I'll call her and tell her you'd like a word with her."

"Thanks." Sally stepped away from the desk and walked towards the notice board where the week's menu was pinned in the centre. "Looks like they have decent food here."

"Something to look forward to in our old age, eh?" Lorne quipped.

"I hope not. The idea of staying in a care home at the end of my life has never really appealed to me."

"Me neither. Why don't we make a pact? Agree to always be there for each other in the end."

Sally held up her pinkie finger, and they shook.

A woman in a smart navy skirt suit and low court shoes joined them. "Hello, I'm Lisa Short. How may I help you?"

Sally showed her warrant card and asked, "Is there somewhere we can talk in private, Miss Short?"

"Of course. We can go to my office. It's this way."

They followed her to a room just behind the reception desk.

She sat in her executive chair and invited them to take a seat. "I'm intrigued to have two police officers sitting in my office."

"First, I'd like to thank you for agreeing to see us at such short notice."

"My pleasure. I must say, I'm surprised to see you here. What brings the police to our care home?"

"We're investigating a cold case, crimes that were committed fifty years ago."

Lisa cocked her head to the side. "Okay, what does that have to do with the home?"

"It's more to do with two of your residents."

"Oh my! Who?"

"Denis Styles and Martin Drake."

"Oh, my goodness. What sort of crimes are you talking about?"

Sally could see the fear develop in her eyes as Miss Short picked up a pen and twisted it through her fingers. "The worst kind of crime. Involving innocent members of our society, children."

"No, no, no. You can't come here and tell me that. What should I do about it?"

"Nothing, for now. With your permission, we'd like to interview the two men. Do you think they'll be up to it?"

"Denis might be, but not Martin. He's fading fast. He has dementia. The doctor visited him yesterday and told us the grim news that he believes Martin will only be with us another day or two."

"Shit! That's not what we were hoping to hear. I'm sorry about that. Would it be possible for us to have a quick chat with Denis?"

"I don't see why not. All I ask is that you be gentle with him. He's not in the best of health either. He had a heart attack six months ago and hasn't really been the same since."

"Damn. Okay, I'll take it easy on him. I need to find out if he remembers anything."

"And what if he does? Are you going to arrest him and throw him in prison? I can tell you one thing: he wouldn't last a day in there, and I think it would be wrong for him to be put under that much stress at this time of his life."

"Our job isn't easy at the best of times, and when an investigation of this magnitude comes along, it's a darn sight worse. Let's see how we go during our chat with him, after which I'll decide if we should proceed."

Lisa stared at the wall ahead of her for a moment or two and eventually nodded. "Okay, under one proviso."

"Go on."

"That I attend the interview. I don't think his family would forgive me if I left him alone with you, knowing that he's a very ill man."

Sally shrugged. "I'm not averse to that."

"Let me visit him first. Make sure he's well enough to see you, if that's all right?"

"Absolutely."

Lisa left the office.

"Bugger, not what we were expecting or needed at all," Sally said.

"It would be awful if the man died because of the pressure we put him under, but on the other hand, he didn't think about what he was putting those innocent children through when it was supposed to be his job to protect them."

"You're right, of course. Shit, what a difficult situation we find ourselves in."

Lisa returned to the office to collect them. "He seems a wee bit brighter, so I guess there will be no harm in letting you speak with him."

"We promise not to push him," Sally confirmed.

"Thank you."

They set off through the communal area and along a narrow corridor that led to a beautiful garden.

"Has Styles been a resident here long?" Sally asked.

"About two years."

"What about Drake?"

"Three years or thereabouts. I'm struggling to wrap my head around the crimes they've both committed."

"I'm sorry. I couldn't have gone ahead with the interview without you knowing."

"I wouldn't have let you see him if you hadn't told me," Lisa said, smiling as she stopped outside room ten. "We're here. I don't have to tell you to take it easy on him, do I?"

"No, we've already agreed. Please, I understand your concerns, but you have my assurance that we'll question him sensitively."

"Thank you." Lisa sucked in a large breath and fixed a smile in place, then knocked on the door.

Sally heard a feeble 'come in'. Lisa pushed open the door, and the three of them entered the room. Denis Styles was sitting in an easy chair next to the window, admiring the view of the garden they had glimpsed in the hallway. He smiled at Lisa.

"Hello, again, Miss Short."

"Hello, Denis. It's lovely to see you doing so well. I bet it's nice to get out of bed, isn't it? You haven't been able to do that for a few months. Umm... these ladies are police officers. They'd like to have a brief chat with you, but only if you're well enough to speak with them."

His eyes widened, and his gaze darted between all three of them. Sally offered a weak smile, and so did Lorne.

"They're here to see me? Why?"

They all sat on the chairs the staff had arranged for them, close to Denis. Then Lisa gestured for Sally to reveal the reason behind their visit.

"Hello, Denis. I'm DI Sally Parker of the Norfolk Constabulary. I run the Cold Case Team there, and this is my partner, DS Lorne Warner."

"Right. It's nice to meet you. Why are you here?" He shifted in his seat to get more comfortable.

Sally noticed his eyes were watering. She had a sneaky suspicion he knew exactly why they were there. "It's about Oakridge Hall." She paused to let the name soak in. "We have it on good authority that you used to be a teacher there. Can you confirm that?"

"Er, yes. Many, many years ago. What about it?"

"Forensics and the pathology teams are out there now, and it's shocking what they have found. Can you tell us what went on at the school?" Sally chose her words carefully.

"I know nothing. I taught there, that's all. Anything else that happened there had nothing to do with me," he was quick to add. Sweat broke out on his brow and above his top lip. He removed a cotton handkerchief from his pocket and dabbed at the two areas.

"Are you sure?"

"Yes. I taught there. As for anything that went on there, I know nothing about that."

"Can you tell us who did what there?"

"No, I refuse to snitch on my former colleagues." His hand covered his heart, and his breathing suddenly became laboured.

"Are you all right, Denis?" Lisa asked. She leaned forward and rested a hand over his.

"No. It's my chest. I can't breathe. You're going to have to leave. I can't do this. This has nothing to do with me."

Lisa faced Sally and Lorne and nodded. "I think it would be for the best. It's too much for him."

Sally and Lorne rose from their seats and walked towards the door.

"Sorry, we didn't mean to cause any trouble for Denis. Feel better soon," Sally said.

They left the room and, while they returned to the reception area, an alarm sounded behind them.

"Fuck, don't say Denis has suffered another heart attack," Sally said.

Several staff members rushed past them and barged into Denis' room.

Lisa came out and ran towards them. "We need an ambulance. Now."

The receptionist leapt into action and immediately rang for one to attend.

Lisa leaned against the wall and put her hands on her thighs. "I knew letting you in there to question him would be a mistake."

"I'm sorry you feel that way. In fairness, I barely said anything to him. He reacted as soon as I mentioned Oakridge Hall."

"That was enough. I'm sorry for ending the conversation

so abruptly. I fear he's having another heart attack. I must get back to him." She turned and walked away from them.

A nurse approached her, and Lisa ran into Denis' room again.

Sally, fearing that Denis had passed away, remained in the reception area until Lisa left the room again. Which she did a few minutes later.

Lisa seemed shell-shocked as she walked down the hallway towards them, her shoulders slumped. "He's dead. We did everything we could to save him." Sirens broke the silence outside, and the ambulance drew up at the entrance. "Excuse me, I have to speak with the paramedics."

Sally nodded. "Go ahead. We're sorry it has come to this, Lisa."

"Believe me, so am I," she glared and snapped back.

Sally and Lorne stood aside to allow the paramedics to enter the building with their stretcher, and then they went back to the car. Inside, Sally rested her head on the steering wheel and groaned.

Lorne rubbed her back. "We shouldn't feel guilty about this, Sal. We had a right to interview him."

Sally sat back. "I know, but what if he told us the truth? That he wasn't involved in the torture and the murders that were committed."

"As an outsider, I find that incredibly hard to believe. You should, too. The evidence is there. His name was in that book for a reason. Admittedly, it might not have openly told us who was directly involved with the crimes. You're not telling me there were only three teachers at that school?"

"I suppose there's still a lot of information we need to sift through back at the station. Maybe this was a mistake. Am I guilty of jumping the gun before we have the facts to hand?"

"No, you mustn't believe that. Something good has come from today."

Sally twisted in her seat and asked, "Christ, what?"

"We have Howard Rowe coming in to see us tomorrow. The CPS will be delighted to have one suspect. It's not ideal, but one is better than none, and the families of the deceased will be grateful when they're told the news."

"Your logic can be so off the mark at times."

"What? It's not," Lorne shouted.

"Do I have to spell it out for you?"

Lorne shrugged, her brow wrinkling with annoyance. "Yes, you're going to have to."

"Rowe confirmed that the reason the victims were selected was because they were orphans."

Lorne thumped her thigh. "Of course it was. Sorry, it was stupid of me to forget that information."

Sally reached over and squeezed Lorne's knee. "You're forgiven. It's been a hell of a day. Let's call it quits and head back to the station. We'll stop at the baker's and pick up lunch for the rest of the team."

"Sounds like a good idea. We need something to cheer us up."

Upon their return, the team was just as upset by what had happened as they were. Sally handed around the sandwiches while Lorne poured everyone a coffee. The atmosphere was subdued throughout their lunch.

Sally cleared away the rubbish and clapped to draw everyone's attention. "Right, folks, I know today hasn't been one of the best we've ever encountered, but it's nothing we can't overcome. The positive we need to cling to is that Howard Rowe has agreed to attend an interview with me tomorrow. Hopefully, what he has to say will answer the multiple queries this investigation has thrown up so far. Let's not get distracted by today's events. If anything, it should strengthen our resolve." *What bullshit that is. What did I say that for?* "I'll be in my office if anyone needs me."

She sauntered into her office and rang Pauline. "Hi, can you talk?"

"Just a second. Let me relocate, I could do with some fresh air."

There was a pause while Pauline readjusted her position. Footsteps and heavy breathing filled the line. "I'm here. What do you want, Sally?"

"I was calling to check how things are going at your end. Although I have some news of my own to share."

"You, first."

"Well, from the information that we brought back from the house, we've found three suspects. All teachers who we believe were involved in the torture and murders."

"Okay. Why do I sense a *but* coming?"

"Not one to disappoint you... but we visited two of the men today. One of them lives at home with his very sick wife. He arranged for his daughter to sit with her tomorrow so he can come in for questioning. He didn't want to tell us much without his solicitor being present. However, he told us that things changed at the school when the new headmaster took up his position."

"Interesting. Did he show any remorse?"

"Yeah, it seemed pretty genuine."

"What about the other two men?"

"Ah, yes, there lies a story. We showed up at the care home where they both live. One man has dementia and hasn't got long to live. I decided not to bother him. The manager agreed we could interview Denis Styles, and all was going well until I mentioned Oakridge Hall. He swore to us he wasn't involved in the crimes and then had a heart attack."

"What the fuck? Is he all right?"

"No, he didn't make it."

"Bloody hell. I suppose it was to be expected, given the men's ages. Let's hope you have better luck with the one you're interviewing tomorrow."

"I hope so, too. Have the divers finished?"

"Yes, they packed up and left about an hour ago. You'll be pleased to know that no further bodies have been found in the lake."

Sally blew out a relieved breath. "I am happy about that. Umm... I've got another snippet of news I'd like to bring to your attention."

"Crap, this sounds ominous. Go on, hit me with it."

"Lorne has a friend coming up from London to visit her."

"Is this information important to the investigation? If not, why are you wasting my time with idle chitchat?"

"I'm not. Listen for once in your life, will you?" Sally snapped. "Sorry, I shouldn't have had a go at you."

"Apology accepted. Now get on with what you're trying to tell me before nightfall descends on us."

"Cheeky cow. Anyway, when Lorne was in the Met, she sometimes worked with this lady, and her contribution in solving some cases was second to none."

"Again, can you get on with it? Edit, edit, edit, just tell me the facts and leave out all the other shit."

"Jesus, you can be a pain in the arse sometimes."

"I know. I'm sure Simon showed little tolerance with you when he was in my role, as well, not that you'll ever admit it."

"I would if it were true. It's not. Anyway, I don't wish to

hold you up any longer than necessary; I just wanted to give you a heads-up that we'll be visiting in the morning and bringing Carol with us."

"Why? Who is she? A specialist of sorts? Lord knows we could do with all the help we can get around here, but if she's going to get under our feet, she'll feel my wrath."

"Yes, I'm fully aware of how temperamental you are."

"I'm not. I dispute that. Time's getting on. Are you going to tell me who this bloody person is or are you expecting me to look into my crystal ball when I get home this evening?"

Sally tittered. "You've hit the nail on the head."

"What?"

"She'll probably be up for giving you a few pointers for when you use your crystal ball."

"Will you grow up and stop serving up such cryptic crap? Some of us have important work we need to get on with."

"Rude and unnecessary, but I'm prepared to let you off this time. Carol is a psychic."

"Holy shit. Are you bloody winding me up? Is this your way of getting revenge for me having a go at you?"

"No. It's the truth, the whole truth, and nothing but the truth."

The line went dead.

Gobsmacked, Sally stared at her mobile, and her finger hovered over the keypad, ready to call Pauline back, but she thought better of it and placed her phone on the desk. "Damn woman. Still, nothing she does should surprise me. Fuck, I dread to think what type of reception we're going to receive tomorrow."

"Talking to yourself again?" Lorne asked from the doorway.

"Sometimes when things get too bad, I find it helps. Come in, take a seat."

"Go on, I'll ask. What were you chuntering on about?"

"I've just finished speaking with Pauline."

"Oh no, don't tell me they've discovered more incriminating evidence at the scene?"

"No, nothing else, yet. The divers have packed up and left the location. Thankfully, no further bodies have been found."

"Okay, so what's the problem with Pauline now?"

"I felt it was my duty to inform her we'd be visiting the site in the morning and that we'd be bringing a guest with us."

"And she threw a fit?"

"You could say that. Well... no, actually she didn't. I was giving her the spiel about how influential Carol's powers had been in solving some of your cases down in London, and the bitch hung up on me."

Lorne did her best to hold back the laughter for a second, and then the floodgates opened.

"All right, it wasn't that funny," Sally chastised her before laughing herself. "Okay, maybe it was. I'm not looking forward to the reception we'll probably get in the morning."

"Hey, leave her to Carol to deal with. She loves getting her hands on a disbeliever. She used to wind Pete up something chronic, but now the bloody man won't leave her alone."

"Really? That's hilarious. You don't really talk about him. Are you sure seeing Carol again won't be too much for you?"

"It'll stir up a lot of memories. Hopefully, I'll be able to leave those conversations at home. There are days when I still miss Pete, otherwise known as the idiot."

"You're bound to. You had a great working relationship."

"Not only that, but he was also like a brother to me. He definitely took a piece of my heart with him when he passed away."

"Such a traumatic time for you. You've been through such a lot over the years, I'm not surprised you gave your badge back a couple of times."

"I'm glad you have a supportive DCI because mine sucked."

"And now he's Charlie's boss."

"Indirectly, yes. I think Katie shields her from Sean a lot. Although, from what Charlie tells me, he appears to have mellowed over the years." She chuckled. "Maybe it's less stressful for him now that he doesn't have to deal with me and my shenanigans every day."

"Well, I have never had any cause to complain about your work since the day you started."

"That's great to know. If I'm honest, I had my doubts about whether I would fit in around here, working on cold cases, but I have to tell you, I've loved every second so far. Especially with this case. I know we haven't got very far with it yet but, most of the time, our job comprises of righting the wrongs. This investigation isn't that different to what we'd class as normal or current investigations. The exception is that the tragic events at the hall took place fifty years ago."

"You're right." She rubbed her hands together and smiled. "I can't wait for Carol to visit the house. I know it will tug at our emotions, but it will bring relief to the boys' souls. We need to do it for them."

"It's a shame the author of that letter didn't have the courage to come forward. I dread to think what kind of life he's led over the years, keeping the secrets of that damned school. It makes you wonder how many more former pupils are out there who have also suffered."

"Also, I'm wondering how many other pupils will come forward and reveal their experiences once word gets out about the Forensic Team being out there."

"I agree. I'm currently considering whether to have a conference. Damn, I forgot to ask Pauline if the press had arrived yet."

"If you don't fancy calling her back, the desk sergeant should be able to give you a definitive answer."

Sally smiled and picked up the phone. She rang the front desk to check with the sergeant on duty. "Pat, it's DI Parker. I don't suppose you can tell me if the press has wind of what's going on at Oakridge Hall?"

"I haven't heard either way, ma'am. If you like, I can contact one of the patrols and get back to you."

"Perfect. If you wouldn't mind." She hung up. "He's going to get back to me." The phone rang again after about thirty seconds. "DI Sally Parker, how may I help?"

"It's Pat, ma'am. The vultures are beginning to flock to the site. Currently, there are around half a dozen out there."

"It won't be long before the word spreads and they descend on the area. It might be worthwhile for your men to monitor things and consider sending extra bodies over there to contain the press. You know how industrious these bastards can be. I'd hate to see pictures of that torture chamber plastered on every front page of the nationals."

"I'll get on it right away, ma'am."

"Thanks, Pat. I appreciate it." Sally ended the call.

"What shall we do now?"

"Now that our afternoon plans have been kiboshed?"

Lorne nodded and sighed.

"Go back and start sorting through the ledgers and personnel files," Sally said. "We should see if any other individuals of interest are listed from whom we can gather information. Joanna said the three men we set out to question were the only teachers still alive."

"Yes, you're right. That's two screw-ups in one day for me. There won't be a third, I assure you."

"Something wrong?" Sally asked. She studied her partner, concern rising within.

"No, not really. I keep getting spells of forgetfulness. I don't think it's anything to worry about. Women of a certain age have brain fog to contend with."

"How are you getting on with your HRT?"

"Still getting sleepless nights, and the patches can be a pain in the backside."

"In what respect?"

"They can lose their stickiness and slip off the skin when the body gets hot."

"I thought HRT is supposed to help stop you from dealing with hot flushes?"

"Yes, in general, it does. But sometimes the body sweats naturally."

"Eww... it's not something I've had to think about."

"Let's hope you sail through the menopause. Some women do. My mother was one of them. I don't recall her ever having a hot flush in her life."

"Maybe it skipped a generation. I wonder how our grandmothers and all the women who came before them had to deal with the menopause. It must have been around in those days."

"I've got a theory on that."

Sally inclined her head. "Which is? Or do you intend to keep it to yourself?"

"Centuries ago, they used to burn women for being witches. How do you know that some of those women weren't driven insane by their raging hormones?"

"Christ, you might be on to something there. I've never thought about it in that way before."

"I don't suppose we'll ever get to the truth, because women have always been regarded as second-class citizens throughout history. What the men seemed to forget was that without women birthing their offspring, mankind wouldn't exist today."

"That's pretty profound of you, Lorne."

"But an accurate observation all the same."

"I'll have to take your word for that one. Right, let's crack on. I'd like to get away from here sharpish tonight."

Lorne stood and asked, "Any particular reason?"

"For one thing, I'm keen to see Carol again."

"Can't that wait until the morning? She's bound to be exhausted when she gets here. She's never been the best traveller."

"I'm shocked that you would think I would hound her as soon as she arrives. No, what I meant was that I'm keen to say hello to her again."

Lorne's eyes formed tiny slits. "You might be able to fool some people, not me, missus."

Sally's grin widened as she sent her partner away, clearing the way for her to concentrate on the emails and unopened letters waiting in her in-tray.

"The jury is still out on that one," Lorne cheekily added before she exited the room.

Sally completed her task, then rejoined the others. "How is it going out here?"

"I've got something of interest, boss," Joanna said.

Sally crossed the room to her desk. "What's that?"

"I've been comparing the list of pupils with the missing person database, and I've found two names that match."

"Interesting. How were they classified in the ledger?"

"Both of them had an M next to their names."

"Have you managed to do any extra research? Such as, do the names exist on the electoral roll? Or what about the persons who reported the boys missing? Are they still with us?"

"I'm in the process of doing that now."

"Good luck with it. Thanks for drawing it to my attention." Sally left Joanna and checked how Stuart and Jordan were getting on. "Anything I should know about here?"

"No, boss. We keep coming up with a blank, no matter which route we take."

"Okay, do your best, boys."

Sally settled at the desk next to Lorne's. "Did you hear what Joanna said?"

"I did. Let's hope something comes from that."

The phone rang in Sally's office. "Bloody hell, no rest for the wicked. I'll be right back." She bolted through the door and answered it on the third ring. "DI Sally Parker."

"Sorry, it's Pat, ma'am. I wanted to update you on the current situation at Oakridge Hall."

"I'm listening, Pat. You sound worried."

"That's because I am. Not long after I spoke with you, I sent another patrol to the location. They've since contacted me to tell me that the area is now flooded with press."

"Shit. Talking about tempting fate. Thanks for letting me know."

"You're welcome."

Bugger, not what I wanted or needed. This means we're going to get hounded every time we attend the site unless the weather changes for the worse.

She was about to leave the office when the phone rang

again. Sally returned to answer it. "Hello, DI Sally Parker. How may I help?"

"You should have left well alone," a disguised voice said. "Why did you have to go snooping around out there?"

She threw something at the door to draw her colleagues' attention. Lorne appeared in the doorway. Sally gestured for her to trace the call. Lorne gave her the thumbs-up and rushed out of the room. She returned to her seat and punched her passcode into her phone to set the recorder, then she pressed the speaker on her main phone. "What do you mean?"

"Don't treat me like an idiot, Inspector. We both know what I'm talking about. Why? Why meddle, after all this time? Why couldn't you leave well alone?"

"Who are you? Meet with me. Let's talk about why you have an issue with us being at Oakridge Hall."

"No. Never. You've opened a large can of worms that you're going to live to regret."

"If you have some information for me, please, I'd like to discuss it in person."

"No. You will not ensnare me in one of your traps."

"What traps? I have never set a trap to capture anyone before. What can you tell me about the school?"

"Nothing. I'm calling to warn you to back off."

"Back off? Why?"

"Because it goes deeper than you realise. I've said too much. Be warned, Inspector, or suffer the consequences. We know more about you than you realise."

"Wait. You can't threaten me like that. All I'm doing is my job. Hey, are you listening to me?"

The line went dead.

Sally switched off the recording and darted out of the office. "Tell me you got a trace?"

Joanna shrugged. "Sorry, by the time we set it up, it was too late, boss."

Sally kicked out at the pile of boxes stacked up against the wall beside her. "Shit, shit, shit."

Lorne approached her. "Let me get you a coffee. What did this person say?"

Sally followed Lorne to the drinks area and replayed the recording while her partner made the coffee. "It's important that I inform Simon about the situation, in case they pursue him."

"I think that's a wise move. Shit, what have we uncovered here?"

"More than the proverbial can of worms, judging by what the caller just said. Let's hope Carol can shed some light on it."

"That's going to put a lot of pressure on her shoulders. Do you want to know what I think?"

"I'd love to get your take on it. Go on."

"Maybe this person has a connection with one or both of the teachers we visited today."

Sally adopted The Thinker pose. "Possibly. Thinking outside the box, they might also be connected to the bastards. I mean, some dignitaries who treated the school as a brothel."

"Oh, bugger. You're right. That thought never even crossed my mind."

"Where do we go from here?"

"Our main objective is to keep the team safe, and our families, of course. We're at a loss until we gather the necessary information to identify the perpetrators of these terrible crimes."

"I repeat, unless Carol can help us out."

"It's unlikely to occur unless the spirits guide us to the ones responsible."

"Has that happened before?"

"Yes. But I wouldn't bank on it. Don't forget, Carol no longer has youth on her side."

"I know. I'll try to tamp down my expectations. What we need to do is focus all of our efforts on finding out who those dignitaries are. That's obviously the key, and what is ticking this person off."

Lorne handed her a mug. "I think you're right. I'm also thinking about the headmaster, the person in charge of all this debauchery and shame."

"He's dead, or had you forgotten?"

"No, I know. That's not my third memory slip for the day. What I was trying to get across was whether we could trace his relatives; maybe his wife, or children."

Sally contemplated Lorne's suggestion and nodded. "You're right. You get on with the research, and I'll call Simon." She took her coffee through to her office. Sat at her desk and steadied her breathing for a moment before she made the call.

"Hi, how are things?"

"Are you driving?"

"Yes. What's wrong? Sally, I can tell there's something wrong by the tone of your voice."

"Can you find a convenient spot and pull over? Is Tony with you?"

"I'm here, Sal."

"Yes, you're on speakerphone. I'm pulling into a parking space now."

"Good. I've got something to tell you, both of you."

"Shit! It's not Lorne, is it?" Tony asked.

"No, calm down. No one has been hurt, but I need you both to be aware of something."

"I'm turning the engine off. What is it, love?"

She sighed heavily, and unexpected tears misted her vision. "I'm sorry to scare you like this. I felt it was important for you to know right away."

"We're listening. What are you talking about?" Simon asked, his anxiety getting the better of him.

"It's the investigation we're working on. I've just had a call from someone who felt it was necessary to disguise their voice, which immediately put me on the back foot."

"And? What did they say? Did they fill in any of the gaps for you?"

"No, in fact, quite the opposite. They warned us off. My immediate thought was this person might come after either you or Tony."

"Did they come right out and say that, Sal?"

"No, but the warning was there all the same. They told me they know more about me than I realise."

"Shit! Okay, we get the message loud and clear. We'll keep a watchful eye out as we're driving around, visiting our sites."

"I'm asking you to consider upping your security on the sites."

"Excellent idea. Leave it with us. And, Sally?"

"Yes."

"Make sure you practise what you preach and up your personal security as well, you hear me?"

"Loud and clear. Don't worry, we're both on the same page there. I love you both. See you later."

Both men shouted that they loved her back, which brightened her day. However, the feeling didn't last. She returned to let Lorne know about the call.

"I had to make them aware. They're going to remain vigilant. We all need to be aware of what's around us, folks. Don't be blasé about your security when you're not at work."

The team nodded their agreement.

Sally covered her face with her hands and groaned. "Why do I have a sense of doom hanging over me?"

Lorne rubbed her forearm and said, "Push it aside. The call was bound to have a devastating effect on you. That was the caller's intention; for you to question yourself. Don't let them win."

"I know you're right. Okay, this is me pushing it aside. What have you found out about the headmaster's family?"

Joanna raised her hand. "I've been digging in the archives, and Frank Gorman's name doesn't surface until after his death."

"What do you mean?"

"There's nothing. No placements at other schools," Joanna said.

"And after his death?"

"I found some articles in the local newspaper featuring pupils from a previous school where he worked in Southampton speaking out about him."

Lorne picked up her pad and pen. "What's the name of the school?"

"Wyfield Secondary School. I've checked, and it closed down decades ago because of the number of abuse cases that were highlighted around that time."

"So, what are we saying here? That he was feeling the heat down in Southampton so moved to Norfolk instead, where he spread his disgusting sadistic ways at Oakridge Hall?"

"So it would seem," Joanna replied.

Sally closed her eyes and inhaled a breath to calm her

racing heart. "And these dignitaries helped to cover up what was going on there? It beggars belief that this investigation has gone from bad to worse today. Was he married?"

"Yes, one article mentioned his wife's name as Anna. I'm trying to find an address for her now," Joanna told her.

"Stick with it. Come on, folks, let's dig deeper than we've ever dug before during an investigation. To the bloody southern hemisphere, if we have to."

"Hang on, I might have something here," Joanna announced.

Sally approached her and checked out her computer screen over her shoulder. "What have you found?"

"On the electoral roll, I have a Jane Anna Gorman. That might be her."

"Either she changed her name, or she's chosen to use her middle name over the years. Her address?"

"Sixteen Broad Street in Hethel."

Sally patted Joanna on the shoulder and straightened up. "Come on, Lorne, get your coat. We'll shoot over there now and see if she's willing to have a chat with us."

Lorne slipped on her coat, and Sally removed hers from the coatrack in the corner.

"Excellent work, people. Keep it up while we're out. We'll be back soon, hopefully."

6

They arrived at the small bungalow on the edge of the village.

A woman in her eighties was planting a large shrub in the front garden. She stopped and glanced their way when Sally and Lorne entered the gate. "Can I help you?"

"Hello. I'm DI Sally Parker, and this is my partner, DS Lorne Warner. Are you Jane Gorman?"

"I am. What do you want?"

"Was your husband Frank Gorman? Previously the headmaster of Oakridge Hall?"

Mrs Gorman lifted her head and eased the tension in her neck. "He was." She peered over her shoulder and said, "You'd better come inside. I'll just tidy up here first. I wanted to get the gardening finished before the next spell of rain hits us. It's been vile the past six months, hasn't it?"

"You're not wrong. Summer was a definite washout. Can we help?" Sally offered.

"That would be wonderful. I'll put most of it in the

wheelbarrow if one of you wouldn't mind pushing it around the back for me."

"I'm sure we can manage that."

Mrs Gorman placed a spade and fork, along with her gardening gloves, in the wheelbarrow, which already contained a bag of compost, and then stood back.

Sally smiled and grabbed the handles. "If you'd like to lead the way?"

They followed the woman up the path at the side of the house and paused as she opened the gate, revealing a large garden that was well-stocked with shrubs and trees but lacking in colour due to the time of year.

"Just leave it there. It should be safe. I can unload it and put it in the shed later, after we've had our chat. Would you like a drink? I was about to make myself a cup of tea, so it's no bother."

"Thank you. We both prefer coffee if you have any?"

"I do. Come inside. Don't worry about taking your shoes off. Mopping the floor is on the agenda for later. I thought I'd do some gardening first."

Once inside the dated kitchen, she busied herself preparing the mugs and invited them to take a seat.

No one spoke until she distributed the drinks and joined them at the table. "Now, what's this all about?"

"I'm not sure if you're aware, but the Forensic Team has been searching Oakridge Hall this week," Sally said tentatively.

"Really? No, I hadn't heard. Has it been on the news?"

"Not yet, but it's only a matter of time, judging by the amount of press who have assembled."

"May I ask why? After all this time?"

"I received an anonymous letter at the start of the week.

It was agreed that we, as a Force, should act upon the contents of the letter. So SOCO and Pathology were called out, along with a dive team who has been searching the lake on site."

Mrs Gorman's gaze dropped to her mug, and she twisted it on the coaster. "I see, and have the searches they conducted found anything of importance?"

"You could say that. I'm sensing none of this is news to you."

"What are you insinuating?"

"I'm not. All we're trying to do is get to the truth. Were you aware of what went on at Oakridge Hall when your husband was the headmaster there?"

Silence filled the room for several moments. Sally felt that Anna Gorman was searching for the right words to say. "Mrs Gorman? Were you aware?" Sally repeated.

"Please, call me Jane, or Anna, if you prefer. I don't mind."

"Did you change your name after the story appeared in the papers?"

"I had to." She broke down in tears.

Sally faced Lorne and asked, "Have you got a tissue?"

Lorne shook her head. "Sorry, not today. I changed coats this morning."

Sally spotted a roll of kitchen towel and left her seat to fetch some. She handed two sheets to Anna. "Here you are. I didn't mean to upset you."

Anna separated the sheets, blew her nose on one and wiped her eyes with the other. "It's not your fault. You being here has brought all the memories flooding back to me. I was in pieces when my husband finally revealed the truth about what he'd been up to and what was going on at the school. I had to block it out, shut it away in that little safe in my mind, otherwise I would have gone crazy. Now, it seems all those images has been set free again. I'm not sure how I'm going to cope this time around. It was so hard to store them away fifty years ago, but somehow, I managed it." She broke down again.

Sally swallowed down the lump bulging in her throat. "Please, we're not here to cast any aspersions on you, or to blame you for your husband's behaviour. However, we are eager to know the truth about what took place at Oakridge Hall."

Anna dried her tears, met Sally's gaze and confessed, "It was all a cover-up. Dozens of depraved men visited that school at night to do unspeakable things to those children. I remember the night my husband finally sat me down to reveal the truth after years of denial. Little did I know that when I woke up, I would find him dead beside me. He\d had a heart attack."

"I'm sorry you had to put up with that sort of behaviour. Would it be wrong of us to ask you what he told you? The investigation is still in the initial stages, and despite the Forensic Team discovering several bodies at the site, we're struggling to find out what happened to the boys who died."

Anna's mouth dropped open for several seconds. She stood, collected the roll of kitchen towel from its spindle and returned to the table. She tore off another couple of sheets and repeated the process she'd carried out previously. "He told me everything. It was so awful." The tears flowed again.

Why the fuck did she keep this to herself? She might now face charges for withholding information about crimes. Sally reached out for the woman's hand. "I'm so sorry to put you through all this pain and anguish, but we need to get to the truth, and I think you're the only person who can share that with us."

"Thank you. Maybe if I did tell you, it might rid me of the images once and for all. Who knows if I'll be successful in locking them away a second time, at my age?"

"Whatever you think is for the best."

"I can tell you one thing: my husband was an evil monster, but he always hid that side of himself at home. If he hadn't, I suppose he knew what the consequences would have been. I would have left him without a moment's hesitation."

"I can tell you're a very strong woman, Anna."

"I wasn't the day he confessed. He must have known that he wouldn't be around to deal with the shock and my reactions once the news sank in. I was struck dumb and listened to him attentively, with tears streaming down my cheeks, of course, but he had no idea how much hatred was building inside."

"Was he remorseful throughout?"

"No, he showed little to no sign of remorse. When I went to bed that night, I wished he were dead. You can't even imagine how I felt the next day when he didn't wake up. I had to live with that guilt for years. The truth is, I had nothing to feel guilty about. He did. I have never missed him. Yes, I went through a period of grieving, but I don't think it was specifically for him. I believe it was for the children he'd used, abused, and ultimately killed."

"Do you know who some of these dignitaries were?"

"Yes, I was appalled when he told me. Some of them were high-ranking officers at your station and in Norwich. Members of the county council, solicitors. Men with successful jobs, men I would never have believed could carry out such heinous crimes. Tempted as I was to reveal the truth, I knew it would be brushed under the carpet by the police. Similar to a lot of crimes like this back in the day. We all know what a scumbag that Jimmy Saville was. Look how many years he got away with it, right under our noses. The BBC should be ashamed of themselves. There's another case similar to that in the news right now, isn't there? It's appalling how these men think they can get away with... I can't say it. They're bastards, well, most of them. I know the statistics will back me up, too."

"I agree. During the seventies, eighties, and even part of the nineties, it was easier for men to fulfil their fantasies with children. Nowadays, not so much, but like every crime, there will be those who believe they are above the law, only to be found out in the end."

"It's shameful, degrading as a woman to know that I wasn't enough to satisfy my husband's needs."

"No, you need to stop thinking that way. Whether these men had happy marriages is irrelevant to what they were doing. It's how their brains were wired. The less said about that, the better."

"I agree. All I know is that if the truth had come out, it would have disgraced my family, what was left of it at the time."

You selfish cow! What about those children? "Do you have any children?"

"We had a son. He died when he was five. He ran into the road while we were having a family day out. We called an ambulance, and he was rushed to the hospital. Sadly, he never made it and died en route. Another reason why I wouldn't have been able to forgive Frank."

"Maybe that was the trigger," Sally suggested.

"No, please don't say that. I can't bear to think that's the reason he went off the rails."

"Did Frank admit to abusing your son before he died?"

"No. Had he told me he'd laid a finger on Adam, I would have killed him myself."

"Anna, we need you to give us a statement."

"What? After all this time?"

"Yes, after all this time. Your testimony is crucial to our investigation. It will strengthen our case, and ensure these men face justice."

"But what's the point now? What would it achieve?"

"It will expose the truth. And we will finally be able to get justice for the boys who were brutalised."

Anna's brow wrinkled. "Most of the people responsible are already dead. How do you plan on getting justice?"

"Some are still alive. Those are the ones we need to hold accountable. And your statement could be the difference between them walking free or paying for their crimes."

Anna sighed, visibly shaken. "I never thought I'd be in this position. I'm not sure if I'm ready. Can I think about it?"

"No, Anna. This isn't something you can sit on any longer. Children suffered because of what happened, and some of the men responsible are still out there. I understand this is difficult, but the longer you wait, the longer justice is denied."

Anna looked away, tears brimming. "But if I do this, people will hate me. They'll judge me for staying quiet for so long. What about the families of the men involved? It would destroy them."

Sally's voice hardened. "And what about the families of those boys? They've been living with unanswered questions and unimaginable pain for decades. You have a chance to finally bring them some closure. But only if you're brave enough to act."

Anna buried her face in her hands. "I feel trapped. No matter what I do, I'm going to be judged."

"We're not here to sugarcoat things. Yes, this will change your life, but doing nothing keeps you complicit in their suffering. You have to decide whether you're willing to live with that."

After a long pause, Anna looked up. "Give me some time. I need to sort through this in my own head."

Sally held her gaze. "I'll give you time, but not forever. Those children deserve peace, and every day that passes without action is another day that peace is denied."

Anna nodded, subdued. "I'll think about it."

Sally handed her a card. "Contact me when you've made your decision. But don't take too long. Justice doesn't wait."

As they left, Sally turned to Lorne. "I pushed her, but it needed to be done. We can't afford to let her sit on this any longer."

Lorne nodded. "She'll come through. Her conscience won't let her stay silent forever."

Sally sighed. "I hope you're right."

"We won't know the answer to that until she contacts you. I wouldn't beat yourself up about it."

"How would you have handled it if you were in charge?"

"Pretty much the same way."

"Pretty much?" Sally pushed.

"You've given her the option. I don't think her conscience will allow her to let us down, love."

"I hope you're right. She seemed a nice lady. I think the subject being raised shocked her more than she anticipated it would."

"It must have been awful. I mean, when he revealed the truth, all those years ago. In some respects, I feel sorry for her, having to lock the images away for all these years."

"And now they're probably swimming in her head, and that's down to me. But she should have come forward."

"Down to us, and yes, she was wrong not to break her silence. Our consciences should be clear, we're only doing our job, which means seeking the truth and getting justice for the souls those disgusting men destroyed."

Sally started the car and pulled onto the main road. "I couldn't have lived with that knowledge in my head all these years." Her phone rang, putting an end to their conversation. She answered it through her car navigation system. "Hello, DI Sally Parker. How may I help?"

"Inspector? It's Anna Gorman."

"Oh, hello, Anna. I wasn't expecting to hear back from you so soon. Is there something you forgot to ask me?"

"No. I'll do it. I've thought about your request and, you're right, we need to do all we can to ensure those children now rest in peace. Where do we go from here?"

"I can't thank you enough for your willingness to do this for us. I'll arrange for an officer to come out and see you. I'll get them to call you first."

"Can you arrange for a female officer to come? I'm not sure if I could reveal what I know to a man."

"I agree. Leave it with me. Thank you again for doing the right thing."

"Hopefully, it will help your investigation and allow you to bring it to a close sooner. I've just thought there is a box in the attic. Paperwork relating to the school that my husband told me not to mess with."

Sally slammed on the brakes and faced Lorne. "Oh God, seriously? We'll turn around and come back to take a look, if that's okay?"

"Feel free. I'll leave the front door open for you."

"Thank you, Anna. We'll be two to three minutes."

"I'll open the attic for you."

"No, please, we'll sort that out when we return."

"Very well. Thank you."

"We'll see you soon." Sally ended the call and then completed a three-point turn when a gap appeared in the traffic.

"Bugger! Did you have to do that? Couldn't you have reversed into a side road up ahead?" Lorne asked.

Sally straightened the steering wheel and grinned. "Possibly."

Lorne peered out of the side window and mumbled something.

"Sorry, I didn't catch that," Sally said. "What did you say?"

"You weren't supposed to hear it. Just get us there in one piece, please."

"Your wish is my command. Hey, don't be so grumpy."

"I'm not. I'm thinking."

"About?"

"The investigation, of course."

Sally turned right at the end of the road and drew up outside Anna's bungalow again.

Anna opened the door and seemed pleased to see them. "I've got the ladder ready for you if one of you ladies wouldn't mind going up there for me. My ladder-climbing days are long over."

"I'll do it," Lorne volunteered.

"That's a relief," Sally said. "I hate attics at the best of times."

Lorne climbed the ladder. Pausing briefly, she moved the small door aside, before resuming her journey. "Good job I'm wearing trousers."

They all laughed.

Lorne disappeared out of sight, then reappeared again to ask, "Sorry, I should have asked, which direction should I be going in? Because there are quite a few boxes up here, Anna."

"Oh no, it's my fault. I should have told you. Along the back wall, there's a box that is taped up and has the word 'private' written on the top."

"Thanks. I'll try to find it."

Sally held on to the stepladder and peered through the gap, her ear trained on what was happening above. Lorne grunted and uttered an expletive.

"Are you okay?" Sally asked.

"Yes, it's a bit heavy. I might need to unload some of it before I try to move it."

"Wait, I've got another couple of boxes in the garage. I'll get them for you."

"Did you hear that, Lorne?"

"I did. I'll start unpacking and pass the contents to you, Sal."

"I'll climb up and meet you."

Anna returned with two extra boxes and placed them behind the ladder.

"We're ready down here." Sally ascended the steps, holding on tightly. She hated heights as much as she hated attics. "I'm here."

Lorne carried several books towards Sally. "Are you going to be all right?"

"I'm not sure. I don't feel safe. Maybe we should leave them there and you can pass them down to me when I'm on solid ground."

Lorne tutted. "You're hopeless, but yes, that makes more sense."

Sally's knuckles turned white as she began the journey

back down the metal rungs. She released a sigh once she'd reached the floor. "I'm back down and in one piece."

Lorne laughed and continued to ferry the books back to the opening. "All done. I'll get into position and hand them to you."

"I'm ready and waiting."

They transferred the books to the new boxes, and Lorne closed the door to the attic. She jumped off the ladder and wiped her hands together, sweat beading her brow.

"How was it?"

"Exhausting and scary. I had to have a word with myself. Job done now. Shall we go?"

"Do you need a hand putting the ladder back, Anna?" Sally asked.

"I'll be fine. You ladies get off. I hope the information helps."

"Thank you. I forgot to mention that we've already found several secret rooms at the school. One was an office. My team is going through all the paperwork found as we speak."

"Goodness me. The plot thickens, doesn't it? I wonder what you'll discover in these books, then."

"We're about to find out. Again, thank you for your help."

"You're welcome."

Sally and Lorne picked up a box each and transferred them to the boot of the car, then headed back to the station.

"I'm eager to find out what the books are going to reveal," Sally said.

They unloaded the car and entered the station. Pat rushed to assist them.

"We're fine. Thanks for offering, though. You can open the security door for us, if you would?"

Pat punched in the code, and Sally and Lorne carried the boxes up the stairs and into the main office. They added them to the pile of boxes close to Lorne's desk.

"I'll make a start on them now," Lorne said.

Sally brought the rest of the team up to date and explained the boxes they had returned with. Then she joined Lorne, and they spent the rest of the afternoon flicking through them.

"They're accounts, and he's squirrelled the money away in offshore accounts," Sally said. She shook her head in disgust. "I bet Anna has no idea how much money he stashed away. Of course, if we can get it back, the money will probably be divided between the CPS, the Home Office and the police."

"Don't forget a portion might go to the victims, too. If any of them survived," Lorne was quick to point out.

"I'm guessing the person who sent the letter could be classed as a victim."

"Absolutely. We should compare the names in these accounts to the ledgers Stuart and Jordan are examining, which involve the dignitaries."

"I agree. We can pass that task over to the boys in the morning. I've had enough for today. Let's call it a day." Sally leant over and whispered, "And I'm dying to see Carol."

Lorne smiled. "You're incorrigible. She'll be tired and will need her rest this evening if she's going to be any good to us in the morning."

"Spoilsport."

"You do it every time."

"What?"

"Wear me down. You and Simon had better come for dinner this evening."

"Oh, how wonderful of you to invite us!"

Lorne removed her phone from her pocket. "Hi, it's me. Have you picked up the package?"

"Yes, she's been safely delivered and appears to be in good spirits."

"Great. Umm... do you fancy having another couple of guests join us for dinner this evening?"

"Already sorted."

"What do you mean?"

"Simon's knocking up a meal for all of us, dinner at their place tonight."

"Nice swerve. I'll pass on the good news to Sally. We'll be leaving shortly. I'll pop home first to get changed."

"Okay, we'll wait for you here, then. See you soon."

Sally sighed and scratched her head. "Judging by what I overheard, I take it we're doing the entertaining tonight."

"Works for me. It was Simon's idea. Tony jumped at the chance. He'd be foolish not to. We're all aware of what a fabulous chef Simon is."

Sally wiggled her eyebrows. "Why do you think I married him? And he's got an impressive..."

Lorne held her hand up. "Steady on."

Sally tutted. "I was going to say he's got an impressive wine cellar, to boot."

"Ah, phew, I thought I'd better stop you from revealing naughty bedroom secrets."

"No worries on that score. Come on, let's get out of here."

Sally dropped Lorne off at five-thirty. With dinner planned for seven, Sally had ample time to take Dex for a walk by the river. She didn't bother changing but checked in on Simon before she headed off. "Can I help with anything before I go?"

"No. It's all in hand. I had to stop off at the butcher's on the way home, so Dex missed his afternoon stint at the park. He'll probably be crossing his legs by now."

"Ooh, what have we got for dinner?"

"Roast lamb. Tony told me it's Carol's favourite."

"You're so thoughtful. Thank you for putting on a lovely spread for us tonight. I won't be long."

"Take your time. I can get the table laid while I wait for the meat to cook."

"What would I do without you?"

"Starve," he replied with his usual answer.

She blew him a kiss and called Dex. He skidded to a halt beside her, his tail wagging.

They set off and caught up with a neighbour who was walking in the same direction. The air was fresh, but at least it had remained dry all day.

Sally returned to the house at six-fifteen. She asked Simon again if he needed any help, but he insisted he could handle it and advised her to get ready.

She didn't need telling twice. She ran up the stairs and jumped into the shower. She'd already decided on what outfit she was going to wear, but when she removed the black dress, she wondered if it was too dressy for the occasion, so she texted Lorne to ask what she would be wearing.

Lorne rang her back. "I was intending to wear my jeans. Should I reconsider?"

"I don't know. That's why I'm calling."

"Okay, I'll wear a skirt and jumper. How's that?"

"Suits me. Thanks. See you soon."

Sally chose her navy skirt and a sequined black jumper.

When she entered the kitchen, Simon whistled his approval.

"Stunning."

"Get away with you. Wow, the table looks fantastic. I feel guilty now for not helping you."

"Nonsense. I'm in my element. We haven't entertained like this for a while, so I thought I would go the whole hog."

"You're amazing. How was your day?"

"I reckon it was easier than yours. You look exhausted."

"Damn, should I slap on a bit of make-up?"

"Not wishing to insult you, but maybe get rid of the dark circles under your eyes."

She took two paces towards him and kissed his cheek. "Your advice, not insult, is always appreciated. I'll be right back."

Sally tore upstairs again. She quickly put on a layer of foundation and powder and touched up her eyes and lips. The sound of merriment drew her back downstairs, where she found that their guests had arrived. "Hi, everyone. Carol, it's wonderful to see you after all this time. I can't thank you enough for coming to our assistance."

They shared a hug.

"I'm happy to help, Sally. You look fabulous, even with dark circles under your eyes. You needn't have covered them up on my account."

Sally and Simon glanced at each other and burst into laughter.

"Wow, okay, that was spooky."

Carol winked at her. "Can we eat before you ask any questions? I'm starving."

"No questions tonight, I promise. This evening is about us having a catch-up. I mean it, it's so lovely to see you."

"Sal, can you sort out the drinks while I serve up?" Simon asked.

"My pleasure. Does everyone want a glass of red wine?"

Their guests all agreed and then took their place at the table. Sally joined them a few minutes later with their drinks. Simon placed the leg of lamb in the centre of the table, along with the roast potatoes and two bowls of vegetables.

"My, this is a fabulous feast. Thank you for going to all this trouble for me. It's appreciated," Carol said, the colour rising in her cheeks.

"Did you have a good trip up on the train?" Sally asked.

Simon carved the lamb and passed around the plates; then everyone took their turn to serve their vegetables.

"The trip itself was okay, no holdups. I tried to have a nap on the way, but spirits surrounded me. I've never experienced that, not on a train before. Once or twice when I've hopped on a bus. To be honest, I found it quite unnerving to begin with. It's not like I could have tapped the other passengers on the shoulder to tell them that Auntie Grace or Uncle Albert were there, watching over them." Carol chuckled and set everyone else off.

"I guess so," Sally said. "It must be awful to experience that day in, day out, Carol."

"It has its upsides. Pete sends his regards, Lorne and Tony."

Lorne raised a glass. "Still watching over me, partner, after all these years."

One of the kitchen cupboard doors sprang open, and a packet of crisps fell out.

The group all stared at each other.

Lorne stood to investigate what had fallen and laughed

until tears ran down her face. "This flavour was his favourite."

"I knew he would show you a sign tonight, Lorne. It rarely happens. But he's been present for a few days now. If anything, he told me you would need my help, our help, with this investigation. He's been rounding the victims up for me, assuring them that justice would be served."

Lorne returned to her seat with tears in her eyes and whispered, "I miss you, Pete."

Carol reached over and laid her hand on Lorne's. "He's always with you. You should take comfort in that, love. He's refused to leave you all this time."

"I'm grateful for him watching over me, over us."

"Dig in, folks, before it goes cold," Simon instructed, giving Sally a sideways glance.

She nudged him with her knee under the table, and he fixed the smile on his face once more.

The evening turned out to be a phenomenal success. Laughter and tears filled the room until Carol announced at ten o'clock that she had to go to bed after her tiring journey.

Simon loaded the dishwasher, and Sally saw their guests out of the back door, so they could make their way home through the garden.

"I hope it's not too boggy out there for them," Simon said. "Maybe they should have taken the long way around instead."

"You worry too much. They'll be fine. That was a fun evening. Thank you for making a special effort with our meal tonight. It was superb as usual."

"The pleasure was all mine. Dex, you need to go in the garden, boy, and then I think we'll go to bed, yes?"

"I think so. It's been a long day, and I think, by the

sounds of it, tomorrow is going to be an emotional one for us to contend with."

"Sounds like it. Fancy Pete still being around. Watching over Lorne, after all these years."

"That brought tears to my eyes, especially when the crisps fell out of the cupboard. If I hadn't been a believer before, that incident would have altered my opinion. Carol is an amazing lady. It must be so draining for her, dealing with the spirits, seeing them all around her on public transport et cetera. Not something that would appeal to me."

"I have to agree. It would freak me out, as well. I can't explain it, but I feel safe with her."

"I get where you're coming from. She certainly exudes a sense of calm."

7

Sally picked up Lorne and Carol at eight-thirty the following morning. "How are you both?"

"I'm all right, but Carol didn't get a good night's sleep at all. I found her downstairs making a drink at four this morning."

"I'm sorry I woke you, Lorne."

"You didn't. I was awake myself. I had to nip to the loo and saw the light on in the hallway."

"I know, it's so difficult having strangers wandering around your house in the middle of the night."

"You're not a stranger and you didn't wake me. So stop stressing about it."

Sally glanced in her rear-view mirror and asked, "Why couldn't you sleep, Carol? Or is that a silly question?"

Carol smiled. "The latter, Sally. We have such a lot of work to do today. What are your intentions?"

"I was going to stop off at the station first thing, but I'm willing to go with what you want today. So, if you want to visit Oakridge Hall first, that's all right with me."

"Yes, visiting the hall before we go to the station would be preferable."

"That's what we'll do then. I'm not going to prewarn Pauline, we'll just show up. I want you to know that I didn't get a friendly response from the pathologist when I mentioned you were visiting the other day."

"Don't worry, I've dealt with several sceptics over the years, haven't I, Lorne?"

"Yes, one or two we could mention," Lorne agreed.

"It really doesn't bother me what other people think of my abilities. I do it because it brings comfort to friends and family members who are still with us. Like I said last night, Pete should have gone over to the other side by now, but he's a determined bugger and prefers to hang around, watching over Lorne, although most of the time he's with me, bugging the life out of me."

They all laughed, and a black cat suddenly ran out in front of them. Sally had to slam on the brakes.

Carol chastised their spirit companion. "Stop it, Pete. Behave your-bloody-self."

Sally glanced at Lorne and chewed her lip. "Shit, that was a close one."

"Let's hope he has got nothing else planned for us," Lorne replied.

"I've warned him about his behaviour. He's just keeping us on our toes," Carol said.

Sally sighed and pressed her foot down on the accelerator. "He's doing that all right."

Ten minutes later, they drew up outside the gate posts of Oakridge Hall. Carol wanted to get out of the car there and have a wander around the grounds before she ventured inside the house. Sally and Lorne remained in the car.

"How do you think this is going to go today?" Sally asked.

Lorne peered over her shoulder to check on Carol. "I don't know. She was restless during the night. I'd hate to live in her world. Seeing first hand the atrocities that the victims had to endure before their deaths."

"Don't even go there. Our job is bad enough at times, but all we see is the after-effects of the crimes. Can you imagine living through the crimes as they happened?" Sally swallowed down the bile filling her mouth. "I hope we don't find the next couple of days too harrowing."

Lorne placed a hand on Sally's thigh. "Stay strong. I've been through this process several times. I wouldn't say I'm used to it, but I'm going to find it easier than you. Take a step back now and again, if you need to, and I'll take the strain."

"Thanks, partner. I don't know how I'm going to feel when Carol starts telling us how the kids died. I know we have a rough idea, but if she shares all the gory details…"

"She won't go that far. She'll tell us what she believes is necessary for the investigation but will stop short of going through the emotions the children had to tackle at the time of their deaths. Well, that's the experience I've had with her before. She's coming now."

The back door opened, and a concerned-looking Carol slipped into the seat.

"Those poor children. Don't tell me how many souls they've uncovered, don't tell me anything. I'm warning you now, there are dozens of bodies here. Different ages. Did this place used to be a hospital, as well?"

"It did. During World War Two, it was a makeshift hospital."

Carol closed her eyes and shook her head. "They didn't cure people. The men who were badly injured during the war suffered terribly at the hands of a wicked doctor. His father was German, and no one knew at the time."

Sally and Lorne both twisted in their seats and stared at her.

"A German doctor? What the...? Shit, we had no idea."

"I don't think the truth has ever come out."

"Could that be what the torture room was initially used for?" Lorne suggested.

"I think you're right," Carol said. "The equipment was then used on the kids. That's how all this began. The men who tortured the boys thought it would be fun until one of them died and then it spiralled out of control. Worse men were brought here, once word got out, and that led to more kids dying. The images I'm receiving are sickening. No child should go through what they were subjected to. Depraved individuals obtaining sexual gratification at its worst. My skin is crawling, literally." She scratched at her forearms.

"Calm down, Carol. I've never seen you this agitated before," Lorne said.

Tears dripped onto Carol's cheeks. "It's horrendous. Kids as young as eight spent their lives in fear, not knowing if they would be the next to be chosen."

Sally held a hand to her mouth. "Oh God, don't. I don't think I'm going to cope with this."

"You've got to, Sal. The kids need us. Justice needs to be served," Lorne said.

Sniffling, Sally said, "I know we have to do it, but even now, after only a few minutes, my stomach has tied itself into knots and the emotions are welling up."

Carol placed a hand on Sally's shoulder. "I'm sorry, but the truth needs to come out. It has been suppressed for over fifty years, more in the cases of the patients who suffered at the hands of that despicable doctor. He had help from some of the nurses. He was... how shall I put this? Umm... shagging several of the nurses on the understanding that they remain quiet. Some patients died, men who had no living relatives."

"That's similar to what we've found out about the boys," Sally chipped in.

"I know," Carol confirmed. "The patients' bodies are buried in a building within the grounds." She squeezed her eyes shut to help her focus. "It looks like some kind of tunnel underground. Is that possible?"

"Yes, a member of our team found an old air-raid shelter close to the house. We haven't gained access to it yet."

"That's it. You're going to find up to ten bodies in there, some buried, others left to die from the wounds."

"Oh my God, you're kidding?" Sally said, sadness overwhelming her.

"I'm sorry, it's the truth. You mustn't get upset, dear. Their souls have found a better place to rest."

Sally couldn't stand sitting in the car a moment longer and exited the vehicle. Lorne joined her after a few minutes.

"Are you all right?"

"No." Sally sobbed. "I don't think I'm ever going to be all right after hearing what we've heard already."

Lorne hugged her, and they both shed more tears.

"You're going to have to get through this." Lorne handed her a tissue. "I thought we might need these today."

"I didn't expect it would be like this, Lorne. I'm not sure I can go on."

"You can and you will. Do it for the victims. Come on, we need to get on with this. Don't forget we've got Howard Rowe coming in to see us today."

"Shit, shit, shit! I had forgotten. We're going to have to

leave here at ten-forty at the latest to get back to the station in time."

"I'm telling you now, Carol won't be finished by then, and there's no way she'll want to leave this place until she's freed all the spirits and sent them on their way."

"Would you stay with her? I could ask Stuart to attend the interview with me."

"That makes sense to me. Of course I'll stay here. Are you up to carrying on now?"

"I think so. Sorry to be such a wuss."

"You're not. All this is new to you. We knew we were going to be in for a tough day."

Sally inhaled a large breath to help steady her nerves. "I'm okay now, I think. We need to get a technician to search the air-raid shelter."

"That needs to be a priority now. Bloody hell, ten or more bodies down there? It's mind-blowing that a doctor could do that to one patient, let alone ten of them."

"Let's get back in the car and see what Carol can pick up inside the house."

They jumped back in the car, and Sally apologised for her mini meltdown, then drove up to the big house. Pauline was in her van, collecting some equipment. They left the car and walked over to speak with her.

"Hi, Pauline. Let me introduce you to our dear friend, Carol, the lady I was talking about. She's come up from London to lend a hand with the investigation."

"Nice to meet you. I'm going to make it clear from the outset that I'm not happy with you being here, but DI Parker is the SIO on the investigation, and what she says goes."

Carol smiled warmly at Pauline. "Don't worry, dear. I'll keep out of your way. I can already sense many restless souls roaming the hallways here. May I ask how many bodies you've recovered so far?"

"Three in the lake and another six buried behind the walls."

"What? Six? You haven't informed me that more bodies had been found," a disgruntled Sally said.

"You didn't give me a chance. We uncovered another secret room last night. The body count may climb as we delve deeper into our investigation."

"Shit. Okay. Have you got a spare tech we could borrow?"

Pauline looked puzzled. "What do you think?"

"Sorry, it's just that Carol has told us that there might be up to ten bodies in the air-raid shelter we found the other day."

"It'll have to wait. We're concentrating all our efforts on what we find inside the house first."

"Will you allow us to get it open and have a hunt around for ourselves?"

"Feel free. Once you've suited up."

"I'll get an extra patrol team out here. Let them deal with it."

"Do what you like. I must get on. If you intend to come inside, don't forget to put a suit on first."

"Don't worry, we won't. Do we have the all-clear to go everywhere inside?"

"Yes. Just keep out of our way."

"We will."

Pauline brushed past them and entered the house.

"Don't mind her. We have a love-hate relationship. This has nothing to do with you being here, Carol," Sally assured her.

Carol shrugged. "Don't worry about me. I have broad shoulders. I don't expect every professional to understand what I do. Although I'd prefer it if she kept an open mind, at least until I screw up, if I screw up." She smiled and slipped into the protective suit Sally had removed from a plastic bag. "Is it my size?"

"One size fits all," Sally told her, even though she'd chosen a larger size for Carol.

"We'll see." Carol tugged the suit up over her broad hips. "Only just. I bet I rustle when I walk."

"To be fair, we all do that, so you'll be joining the club," Lorne said.

"I'll take your word for that. Right, are you ladies both ready?"

Sally nodded, and her heart rate instantly escalated. "I'm ready. Lorne?"

"I've been ready since I woke up. Let's get in there. No pressure, Carol."

"I know. I'm warning you now, I think you're going to fill that notebook of yours, Lorne."

Sally muttered, "Oh heck," as she guided the others through the main entrance.

As soon as she stepped into the hallway, Carol stopped and tilted her head to listen. "That's strange. The atmosphere is different in here from what it was outside."

"In what way?" Lorne whispered.

Carol held a finger in the air to silence her and closed her eyes to concentrate. "Can you come forward and speak with me? I can hear you laughing. Were you happy here? No? Then why are you laughing? If you don't answer us, we won't be able to assist you."

"Why are they laughing?" Sally prompted.

Lorne shook her head, warning her partner not to be too eager.

It took Carol several more moments of silence before she

said anything. "They won't tell me. Although I've got an image of a grey-haired gentleman who's constantly tired. Hang on, there's more... I think he cares for his wife."

Sally and Lorne stared at each other, amazed by the revelation.

"They must mean Howard Rowe, the ex-teacher who's due at the station this morning for an interview."

Carol nodded. "Yes. Yes. Yes. That's right. Bless them, they're keen to see justice served on the man. A few children died at his hands. He deserves to be sent to prison, whether he's now his wife's carer or not. They're telling me that karma has visited the man, and his last few years haven't been plain sailing, not how he expected his retirement to pan out."

"There's more to come for that man. Can you give me some names of the children he killed?"

"I won't push them, Sally. It needs to be a gradual process. They'll give me the information when they're ready. Can we go to another location now? They're eager for me to see the two rooms that you've discovered."

"Okay, this is where you're going to need to prepare yourself, Carol."

"Don't worry about me. The spirits of these innocent children will guide us and watch over us."

Sally led the way through the hallway and towards the classroom where the first room was revealed.

They came to a stop at the opening of the secret room. Carol gasped, glanced around it, then took a step back and closed her eyes.

"Is that you, precious?" Carol whispered. When she opened her eyes, tears had formed and were on the verge of overflowing. "I'm so sorry he did that to you. You were a brave little soldier. Don't worry, these two ladies will punish the nasty man. Go to your mummy, darling. Justice will be served. Go now, sweetheart."

Sally and Lorne reached for each other's hands. Sally found the scene she was witnessing highly emotional, and a lump the size of a plum swelled in her throat. Lorne rubbed her back, clearly sensing how much it was affecting her. After a while, overcome with emotions, Sally had to exit the room and rushed outside the building to fill her lungs with fresh air.

Pauline found her a few minutes later, leaning against the wall, her hands on her knees. "Oh, I wasn't expecting to find you out here. I thought you'd be conducting a séance with your psychic friend inside."

Sally stood upright and glared at Pauline. "Don't mock her. If you're not willing to accept her talents, then we have nothing more to say to each other." She entered the building again, leaving a gobsmacked Pauline standing there with her jaw dropped open.

She returned to the room to find Carol sitting, exhausted, on one of the old school chairs. "Are you all right, Carol?"

"I will be. As you can imagine, contacting the spirits and conversing silently with them takes its toll on me. That's why I try to hold as many conversations with them out loud. They mean well; it's just me. I'm not getting any younger."

Sally placed a hand on her shoulder. "There's no rush. The last thing we want you to do is make yourself ill. You've already been amazing."

"The boy's name is Michael Cotton. I tried to send him on to be with his mother, but he told me his parents are still alive."

"What? Oh, my goodness. Can Michael tell you their names?"

"Paul and Maria Cotton," Carol told them after a moment's silence.

"Can Michael tell you where they live?"

"Still in Norfolk, at the same house. They were told by the school that he had run away. All right, in your own time, we don't want to push you," Carol whispered to the spirit.

Sally waited patiently for Carol to speak again. "Yes, they're in the same house. He has visited them, but the experience scared his mother, so he didn't try again. He wants them to know that he doesn't blame them for sending him to the school. He loves them and is aware that they tried their best to find him, but the police refused to help."

"What? Can he tell us why?"

"Initially, they set up a small search party, but that only lasted one day. After that, they told his parents that kids run away all the time and that if he wanted to return home, he would, eventually."

"What the...? How awful. What age was Michael?"

"He'd recently had his eighth birthday. That was the last time his parents saw him alive. They took him out to the cinema. They treated him to popcorn and ice cream during the interval. It was the best day ever until they returned him to the school."

"Dare I ask what happened next?"

Carol fell quiet again and nodded. "We won't force you if it's too painful for you to keep going. You tell us in your own time. Can your friends step forward and comfort you? That's good. Come back to me if you want us to know the truth, sweetie. Remember, we're on your side."

Another pause, and then Carol smiled. "We appreciate you talking with us. You know how important it is for us to learn the truth. He will be punished... honestly, you can trust these two officers. I promise they won't let you down."

She nodded and reached out a hand, then slid her other one over the top, leaving a gap in between. "It feels good to touch you, lovely. Remember, your parents loved you. They thought they were doing the best for you." After another pause, Carol whispered, "He punished you for going out with your family? He brought you here. Shackled you and beat you with a whip... I know, love, I can feel the pain you experienced. I'm with you. Be brave, little one." Tears ran down her cheeks.

Sally's heart went out to the older woman, and she squeezed her shoulder to comfort her.

"I'm all right. I want Michael to feel safe with us. It's the only way we'll get to the truth."

"I understand. We appreciate this isn't easy for you, Michael. If you can help us, we can get justice for you and the boys. Help set you free from this awful place," Sally said. She felt foolish talking to the spirit she couldn't see and jumped when something brushed her cheek. She slapped a hand to her face, thinking a spider had come down from the ceiling.

"You felt him, didn't you, Sally?" Carol asked.

Trying to hold back the tears, Sally whispered, "Yes. Thank you, Michael."

"Okay, sweetheart. In your own time. Just to confirm, I'll pass on your message to Sally and Lorne, if that's all right with you... it is, good. You came back to the school at around seven that evening. Mr Rowe met you at the door, told you he had a birthday surprise for you and brought you to this classroom. There used to be a doorway here, leading to this room. The builders came in afterwards and blocked up the opening. Yes... can you tell me more? He said he wanted to play a game with you and thought you'd like being shackled to the wall. He laughed when he slapped the cuffs on your wrists. Then he ripped your clothes off and beat you with a whip. Are you sure it wasn't the cane, love? It was definitely a whip. Your chest was bleeding. He refused to stop, even though you were in a lot of pain. Oh dear, I'm sorry he did that to you. He undid his trousers and forced you to... all right, take your time. You don't have to say anything else. We understand."

Lorne squeezed Sally's hand, and they shook their heads as the tears rose.

"Don't force yourself. I realise how painful this is for you. After he did that to you, did he release you from the shackles?" Carol closed her eyes and sighed. "You were too young to be punished so viciously. I'm sorry you died on your birthday, dear. Especially after you had a wonderful time with your parents that day... Did he leave you there? Did the headmaster know? He did. Was Mr Rowe the only teacher who touched you? Oh gosh, I'm so, so sorry. Three men were guilty: Mr Rowe, Mr Styles and Mr Drake."

Sally and Lorne shared another amazed glance. The boy had named the three ex-teachers they had themselves targeted to speak to, one of whom was dead.

"Does he know about Styles?" Sally asked.

"Do you know, Michael...? You do? How do you feel about that? It's good, but now you have to keep your distance from him. What if he returns here and tries to punish you again? Don't worry, the others will protect you. You leave that to me."

Sally looked at her watch. "I'm sorry, time is marching on. I need to go. Michael, I have to question Mr Rowe now, back at the station. I won't let what he did to you go unpunished."

"He's laughing again, and I'm not sure why," Carol said.

Sally crept out of the room and up the hallway to the

main door. Her phone rang. It was the station. "DI Sally Parker. What's up?"

"It's Pat, ma'am. I wanted to reach out to you and let you know about the situation as soon as possible."

"What situation?"

"We received a call earlier from Howard Rowe's neighbour. I sent a patrol car out to the house. My men found two bodies in the lounge. The front door was wide open."

"What are you saying? Someone got in the house and killed him and his wife?"

"Both of them are dead, no initial signs of forced entry or burglary. Perhaps he left the door ajar so that they would be found."

"Shit! What was the cause of death? Anything found at the scene?"

"A bottle of pills. Maybe he gave those to his wife, watched her die, and then killed himself. He slit his throat. He was found holding his wife's hand."

"Fuck. Sorry for my language. This is the worst news ever. Bugger, bugger, bugger. All right, thanks for the call, Pat. I'll remain at Oakridge for now. Call me if you hear anything else."

"I will. Sorry to be the bearer of bad news."

"It's okay. See you later."

Sally exited the building, hoping the fresh air would help her put things into perspective. The spirits were laughing. Did they know he'd killed himself? With that thought running through her mind, she tore through the house, back to Lorne and Carol.

Carol instantly knew there was something wrong. "You've heard the news?"

"You knew?"

"Not really. When I conjured up the image of Rowe and his wife earlier, their images were fuzzy, almost faint."

"Hang on, what's going on?" Lorne asked.

Sally rolled her eyes. "Pat rang and told me that Rowe and his wife are both dead. He suspects Rowe gave his wife a bottle of pills, made sure she was dead before he slit his own throat. The door to the house was left open so they would be found quickly."

"Holy shit!" Lorne said, her shoulders slumping in defeat.

"Carol, can you ask Michael if that's why the children were laughing when we entered the house?"

Carol didn't need to ask. "That's right, love."

"What else is going to derail this investigation?"

"Sorry," Carol said. "It's okay, Michael. Remember, none of this is your fault, sweetie. I'll protect you. Pete, are you with us? You are, good. Can you help protect the children here from the two evil men who have passed over recently? They've suffered enough at the hands of the men. They deserve to continue their journey. With your help, we can allow them to do that. Thank you, dear man. I knew you wouldn't let me down." She glanced at Lorne and held out a hand for her to take. "Pete's going to be otherwise engaged for a little while, which means for the time being, you're going to need to be extra careful."

"I will be. Thanks, Pete. I know how protective you were of Charlie in her time of need."

Carol nodded. "Yes, he brought her back to you."

Lorne teared up again and whispered, "All this time, I had an inkling he had a protective arm around her."

"He still has. He watches over both of you. That is when he's not bugging the hell out of me in the evenings."

"That's reassuring to know. Thank you both."

"Michael is no longer with us. Can we move to a different area now?"

They relocated.

During their journey, Carol pointed to the classroom they had just passed. "You need to tell SOCO that they'll find yet another secret panel in there."

"More bodies buried in the walls?"

"Unfortunately, yes. I'm telling you, there are dozens here. Longing for someone to rescue them, they have been waiting in a state of limbo for years. They're happy; maybe that's the wrong word to use. They're pleased that someone has finally come to release them. I won't be able to do much in the time I have here, but if you'll have me, I don't mind returning for several weeks, until all the souls have been freed."

"That would be wonderful," Sally said.

"Yes, it would. You can stay with Tony and me. It's always a pleasure to have you come and stay with us, Carol."

"We'll see how far we get first and if I come across anyone standing in my way."

"You mean Pauline?" Sally asked. "Don't worry, you leave her to me. This is our investigation; she hasn't really got a say in what goes on with it."

"I'm telling you now, you're going to fall out about me being here."

Sally shrugged and smiled. "Nothing new there. She can be a cantankerous bugger at the best of times."

"She has personal issues that need sorting before she's willing to trust anyone. She's relatively new to the area, isn't she?"

"That's right. She took over when Simon threw in the towel and retired. Care to enlighten us as to what the issues are about?"

"It's not for me to tell you, but there's a man involved, a father figure."

"Interesting. Thanks for the warning. We'll tread carefully going forward."

"You do that. You'll have to work hard to gain her trust. One minute she can treat you like her best friend, and the next she'll take pleasure in tearing a chunk out of you."

"Spot on with your assessment. I'll take a step back. I'm guilty of poking her with a stick sometimes."

"You need to stop doing that before she puts in a complaint about your attitude towards her."

"Whoa! Consider me warned, thanks, Carol."

Pauline came out of the room in front of them.

"Talk of the devil," Sally muttered.

Pauline wagged her finger. "Not in there. We have too many techs in there as it is, and it's far too cramped to allow anyone else to enter."

"Okay, we can take a hint. In the room back there, second on the right, Carol believes there is another secret panel behind a wall that you might want to investigate further, at your convenience, of course."

"We'll get to it, eventually. We have enough on our hands to sift through right now."

"Fair enough. If you give me some equipment, I don't mind having a poke around in there myself, if it'll help you guys out."

"It won't. You do your job, and we'll do ours."

Sally held her hands up. "Either way is fine by me. Shall we mark the door for you?"

"Despite what you think, Inspector, I'm not stupid. You've already told me which room it is. That should be enough. Now, if you'll excuse me, I need to collect more equipment from the van."

"I could help," Sally offered.

Pauline marched off. "Good grief, if I need your help, I'll ask for it. I wouldn't be too optimistic about that, if I were you."

Sally couldn't help herself; she stuck her two fingers up at the pathologist.

"I saw that," Pauline shouted and rounded the corner ahead of them.

Carol shook her head. "Don't push her. You'll be the loser. Treat her kindly and she'll soon come around. She's been under a lot of pressure since she started her job. A lot of patience on your part is what's called for if you're ever going to have a good working relationship. I seem to remember you and Jacques being at each other's throats from time to time, Lorne."

Lorne's cheeks coloured up. "You're not wrong. We overcame our differences in the end."

Sally grinned. "In the sack, I believe."

"No, not at all. We slept together in the same bed once. Can we move forward instead of constantly revisiting the past? Jacques is gone, I'll never forget him, but I'm with Tony now and I couldn't be happier."

"Here's another thing I kept from you all these years, Lorne."

"Oh God, do I want to hear this?"

Carol inclined her head. "Do you?"

"Sod it, I want to hear it, even if she doesn't." Sally nudged Carol in the ribs.

"Jacques worked his magic to bring you and Tony together. He was with you, watching over you when you travelled to France in search of the Unicorn. Once he saw you hitched up with Tony, he went home."

Lorne was left speechless, which amused Sally.

"I didn't know. Why have you never told me this, Carol?"

"In my defence, I've never felt the right opportunity has arisen to tell you. Plus, in fairness, Tony is with us most of the time, not that I'm complaining."

"Let's get back to work. If this room is off-limits, why don't we show you the office we found in the kitchen?"

"Yes, okay. Why not?"

Sally led the way through the hallway and into the kitchen, where Carol paused as soon as she entered.

"Is something wrong?" Sally asked.

"This room doesn't appear to have changed through the ages. It still bears some similarity to what it looked like when this place was run as a hospital."

"You haven't really told us much about that, and our research hasn't revealed much either."

Carol pulled out a chair and sat at the large wooden table. "I need to rest my weary legs for a while. Let me see what I can come up with." She closed her eyes and rocked back and forth for a few minutes. "This doctor, he used a false name, so I doubt if you would find any records of his employment. It was a different time back then. There weren't the stringent checks that we have today."

"Do you know what his name was?" Sally asked as she and Lorne took a seat on either side of Carol.

"Doctor Whitelaw or Whitlow, I can't get anything clearer than that." She raised a finger and held her head high, as if she were listening intently to someone. "Please come forward. You're amongst friends here. Won't you tell us what you know?" Carol listened and nodded to the spirit reaching out to her. "That's horrendous. You're telling me he experimented on the injured soldiers who returned from the war? Why...? Oh my, yes, I can see now. Were you one of the men he experimented on? I'm sorry you had to endure such treatment. Did he give you a reason why he was treating you so badly? No, you were all in pain, and as far as the authorities were concerned, he was caring for you properly. Okay, you go now. Rest your weary soul."

"What did the spirit say?" Lorne asked.

"He said the doctor treated them as if they were second-class citizens. Left them lying in the beds, writhing in agony, and refused to offer any painkillers. Before his death, he asked the doctor why, and the doctor laughed and told him he wanted to see what the patients' pain thresholds were like."

"Where did this doctor come from?" Sally asked.

"He admitted, just before Eric took his last breath, that Hitler had sent him to punish those who had killed fellow Germans and returned to this country. Eric is one of the bodies in the air-raid shelter."

"How sad. I hope he finds the peace that he's seeking soon," Sally replied.

"He won't find that until his body is discovered and laid to rest, along with the men who stood alongside him in his regiment and died at the hands of this vile doctor."

"How did he get away with it? And if, like you say, there are ten or more bodies in the shelter, how did that happen?"

"One thing at a time, Sally. I'm sure that more spirits who want to come forward will reveal the truth, piece by piece."

8

When they left Oakridge Hall three hours later, Carol was emotionally and physically drained. By that time, the press had arrived. Some reporters recognised Sally and bombarded her with questions that she refused to answer, not because she didn't want to, but because she couldn't, not right now.

"Are you sure you want to continue, Carol?" Sally asked, concerned about her well-being. "You know, going over the ledgers with us? I can take a detour and drop you home if you'd rather do that instead?"

"I'm sure. Now stop worrying about me. I'll be fine if I have something to eat and a short rest."

"Blimey, I forgot all about lunch. We'll stop off at the baker's on the way back." Sally glanced in the rear-view mirror, and Carol had her head resting back with her eyes closed. Sally tapped Lorne's leg and gestured for her to have a peep.

"She's exhausted," Lorne mouthed, not wishing to wake her.

"I'm fine. Will you two stop worrying about me?" Carol insisted, still in the same position.

"Pardon us for caring about you," Lorne said.

"You're pardoned."

They all laughed. Ten minutes later, armed with the team's orders, Sally walked into the baker's to collect their lunch. She came out with two carrier bags full of goodies, which included sandwiches and cakes for the entire team.

After depositing the bags in the boot, she slipped back behind the steering wheel again. "I hope the others haven't eaten."

"You've bought enough to feed an army," Carol said.

"I know two young men who will be determined not to let anything go to waste."

While they ate their lunch, Sally turned the TV on, hoping to hear the newscaster report about the Howes' deaths, but the main bulletin was about Oakridge Hall.

"That didn't take them long. They could have warned me. My hair was a mess." Lorne tried to make light of the situation.

Sally turned up the volume and listened when the three of them appeared on the screen. "Shit! How do they know who Carol is? What craziness is this?"

"Don't worry about it," Carol replied. "We used to get hounded a bit down in London, didn't we, Lorne?"

"After a case, but I don't recall us having any issues with the journalists during a case. This could go one of two ways," Lorne said. She threw her sandwich bag in the bin and stared at the cream doughnut begging to be eaten. "I don't think I can eat that, not yet."

"Then don't. Leave it for later." Sally's phone rang in her office. She darted in there to answer it. "DI Sally..."

"You were warned to back off. You should have left well alone."

Sally recognised the voice as the person who had contacted her the day before. "Tell me why. Who are you?"

She'd raised her voice on purpose, and Lorne appeared in the doorway. Sally gestured for her to trace the call.

"You'll unearth more than you've bargained for. This is your last warning. We know where you live, Inspector, and everything there is to know about your family."

"Is that a threat? If you have an issue with me, let's meet up and thrash it out. Leave my family out of this."

"What? You expect me to meet up with you and get caught in an ambush? Don't take me for a fool, Inspector."

"I'm not trying to. No tricks, I promise."

The phone went dead. Sally threw the handset back in its cradle and returned to join the others. Distracted, she relayed what had happened to the others and then focused on the screen. The camera panned the small crowd that had gathered since they'd left Oakridge Hall. She saw a person skulking at the back, dressed in black with their hood up, who was sticking out like a sore thumb.

"What do you make of this?" Sally pointed out the suspicious person to the others.

Carol and Lorne both stepped closer to the TV to study the person.

"That's the person you need to speak with," Carol whispered. "It's not what you think. They're warning you to steer clear of the property, afraid of what you'll find. One of their relatives was lost in the house. His top priority is protecting his inner peace, driven by the fear of the news spreading and its potential consequences for his relative."

"Shit! Why didn't he just come out and say that?"

Carol shrugged. "It is common for people to perceive the

presence of their relatives in the spirit world, and they often feel overwhelmed by how to manage these encounters. It's the fear of the unknown. That's this man's problem. He believes it would be better to leave the spirits where they are, roaming the school that caused them trouble when they were lads, abused and tortured. He's wrong. These souls deserve to be set free. I can help them get their freedom once the investigation is over. While it may be necessary to make several additional trips to the hall, eventually the truth will emerge, ultimately leading to their freedom."

"But this person has threatened to harm my family."

"They won't. They're playing the 'big I am'. Don't believe them. They haven't got it in them to carry out the threats, Sally. Stay strong and trust me."

"Okay. Shall we get back to it now?"

Carol smiled. "That's my girl. And if we're out that way again later and that person is still lingering in the crowd, we can pull over and have a chat with him."

"Sounds good to me. Thanks for the reassurance, Carol."

Carol and Sally joined Lorne at her desk. Before they got stuck in, Carol wanted to spend time placing her hands over the ledgers.

Sally had a thought and crossed the room to speak with Stuart and Jordan. "What have you found? Anything?"

Stuart picked up his notebook and ran through the details they had stumbled across since Sally had handed over the two boxes collected from Mrs Gorman. Their contents appeared to be accounts. "We've been able to tally up most of the names. The amount some of these sick individuals were prepared to pay 'for being serviced', shall we say, by the kids is mind-boggling. Considering all this happened half a century ago, I reckon some transactions would have bought a two-bedroom house back in the day."

"Oh God, don't."

"I can add something to that if you'll allow me to," Carol called over from her seat.

"Any help you can give us would be brilliant."

Carol closed her eyes and periodically nodded. She covered her face with her hands and wiped away the tears when they emerged. "They held parties for the dignitaries. Hence the vast sums of money involved. These men did unspeakable things to those children, which frequently led to their deaths. The other children were warned that if they ever spoke out, they would be killed, as well. The poor kids didn't have an option but to remain quiet... What's that? You know who contacted the Inspector? Can you tell me who that is? We'd like to speak to him."

Sally thanked Stuart and Jordan and returned to stand by Carol, willing for the information to come through.

"Please, we're desperate to speak with this person. If he hadn't reached out to Sally, the school would have remained stagnant in time. Your souls would still be trapped within its walls. Please, won't you tell us?" Carol crossed her fingers in her lap and waited for the spirit's response. "Billy Trueman. Thank you, thank you. You have no idea how much this means to us. Thank you for trusting us. Can you tell me who Billy is? He was a pupil at the school with you. He was wise enough to escape. When word got out that one child had gone missing, extra security was put in place, so it didn't happen again. Billy was a fortunate boy to have got out of there alive. No, we will never hold it against him. He did the right thing, escaping when the opportunity arose. He's struggling with guilt at the moment. That's why he wrote the letter to the nice inspector. Thank you. Are you going to tell me your name, love? It's Tommy, is it? Tommy Wise, okay, lovely. Are you strong enough to tell us what happened to you?"

Lorne nudged Sally's arm and ran her finger under a name in the book: Tommy Wise. There was a capital K next to it. Sally nodded and sighed.

"Mr Styles, the teacher, he punished you. The punishment went too far, and you were left to die in a locked room, trapped by the shackles. I'm so sorry you had to go through that, Tommy. Thank you for having the courage to come through today, to tell us your story. Your spirit will be set free soon, I promise you. Is there anything else you'd like to add? You didn't have any parents. Your grandfather sent you to the school. He thought he was doing the right thing. He died a few years after your parents and left the money in a trust fund set up for your schooling. But none of the teachers showed any kindness towards the children with no families. They all treated you abysmally. You didn't deserve that. You had a right to be taught lessons, like every other kid in the country. They punished you for the slightest thing possible. You lived on your nerves a lot of the time. School was supposed to be a safe haven for the children. I can't apologise enough for the way those horrible men treated you. Not all adults treat kids like that, love, believe me. You know that's the truth, that's good. Everyone in this room is on your side, seeking justice for you and the other boys who lost their lives at the school. Trust us, we won't let you down, sweetheart."

Carol's unveiling of her conversation with the spirit left Sally captivated.

After the exchange was over, Carol slumped in her chair. "What those kids went through... well, it was horrendous. I'm sorry it's taken Billy so long to reach out for help. If he'd summoned up the courage earlier, then the spirits would have been able to cross over before this."

"We can't worry about that now. Joanna, can you start the search for Billy Trueman? Also check for William Trueman."

"Already started on that, boss."

Sally gave her a thumbs-up. "What a despicable thing to do, to divide the class up if you like. Sifting through the boys who were orphans, effectively treating them like shit while they sat alongside boys with families. None of this makes sense. Why didn't one of the kids speak out?"

"Paedophile rings rarely make sense, Sal," Lorne was quick to point out.

"Ain't that the truth? At least, with Carol's help, we now appear to be getting to the bottom of things. After we've taken care of the school matters, I would appreciate it if you could assist us in gathering information about the hospital, Carol."

"Yes, of course. First things first, though, eh?"

"I agree," Sally confirmed. "Our focus needs to remain with the boys."

"I think I've found him," Joanna called out.

Sally crossed the room to check the information. "Excellent news, thanks, Joanna. Lorne, do you fancy a trip out to see him?"

Lorne's gaze drifted between Carol and Sally. "Now?"

Carol placed a hand on top of Lorne's. "I'll be all right here. I'm surrounded by friends."

Lorne shrugged. "If you're sure, then yes, let's go."

Billy Trueman lived in a small bungalow on a housing estate in Wymondham. Sally inhaled a breath as she rang the bell to his home.

He answered the door and sighed. It was obvious that he had recognised her. "You'd better come in."

They followed him into a small but dated lounge, and on the TV was the news on a different channel than the one they'd been watching at the station. "I'm glad you took me seriously. I've tried to come forward before, but the officers I spoke to didn't want to know. Take a seat."

Sally and Lorne sat on the threadbare sofa, close to his armchair.

"You've tried to reach out before?" Sally asked.

"Yes, every ten years, on the anniversary of my leaving that school. You're the first one to take me seriously and do something about it. They're suggesting on the news that you have a medium or psychic, whatever she likes to call herself, working with you. I'm not into all that mumbo jumbo, but if it works for you."

"She's been exceptional. Without Carol's involvement in the investigation, we wouldn't have made it this far. Carol spoke with Tommy. He wanted to reach out and thank you for always thinking of those boys who lost their lives at the school."

He lowered his head and swallowed. Tearfully, he said, "I did my best. I had to get away from there. I knew Styles had killed Tommy, but who was I going to report it to?"

"You obviously tried over the years; I can only apologise that you weren't taken seriously."

"I know why it is... because it was a huge cover-up. I remember the men in uniforms coming to the soirees, as they liked to call them."

"What type of uniform?" Sally asked.

"Police. I'm not talking bobbies on the beat, as they were back in the day, either. These men were high-ranking officers. That's how the headmaster and all the teachers involved got away with what they did."

Sally shook her head. "It was so wrong. Had we known about this sooner, I would have delved into it straight away. Gone are the days we brush reports like this under the carpet. Were you an orphan when you attended the school?"

"Yes. It was only a matter of time before they 'invited' me to attend one of their soirees. I was too young."

"What age did you have to be to attend?"

"Eight. It was coming up to my eighth birthday. Tommy was eight two days before... before they killed him."

"Can you tell us what happened?"

"Roughly, as far as I can remember, Tommy did something in class. Mr Styles, he was a cruel bastard, one of the worst teachers there. He punished Tommy, forced him on his knees in front of the class. His irritation grew, and Styles marched Tommy out of the room. We never saw him again. Styles tried to tell us that Tommy's parents had come to collect him, as Tommy wasn't feeling very well, but we knew the truth. At least, I did. Tommy had no parents, and he was there because of a trust fund set up by his grandfather."

"Yes, we know."

He frowned and tilted his head, and then it dawned on him. "Sorry, yes, your psychic friend. She must be good then, if that's what she's already revealed."

"She's the best around. Lorne here used to work with her when she was at the Met. We needed the extra help to get to the truth. But none of this would have come to our attention if you hadn't summoned up the courage to write that letter to me. I'm thankful you chose to contact me."

"I'm grateful that you're taking it seriously. Have they discovered many bodies at the school?"

"Not wishing to upset you, but yes, a few. I can't tell you more than that because it's an ongoing investigation."

"I always suspected that Tommy's body was weighted down in the lake."

"What made you think that, Billy?"

"Because they blocked our way, stopped us from walking around it. I was one of those who had an affinity with the water. Tommy and I often strolled around it at the weekends, throwing stones, skimming the water. It was our escape from the rules and regulations forced upon us during the week. It was more relaxed at the weekends... no, it wasn't. What am I talking about? That's when the soirees took place, well, sometimes. No, I'm getting confused. They happened during the week. Sorry to mess you about. I have all these memories, and sometimes they get shifted around in my head. It was such a dreadful time. I've tried many times over the years to lock the memories away, but I've failed dozens of times."

"Please don't worry. Can you tell us what it was like? For you and the other children?"

"Only what I've told you already. It's hard to put into words what those bastards made us do. We'd go to bed at night and feel someone touching us under the blankets. It got to where I expected it. I tensed up, so I was rigid. I always pretended to be asleep, while whoever it was took advantage of me before he moved on to the other boys. Sick fuckers, they were. We didn't have a childhood, not as such. We worked hard during the day and weren't allowed out to play at lunchtime. We had a quick meal of sandwiches and water before getting back to work. Our lessons were varied and had nothing to do with the school curriculum. I couldn't tell you what half the lessons were about. The teachers instructed us on the responsibilities and expectations we would encounter outside the classroom."

"But they allowed you time off at the weekends? Did the boys with families leave the premises?"

"Yes, that's right. The resident boys, or should I say, the orphaned boys, had to remain at the school and weren't allowed to leave the grounds. One or two tried. They were caught and brought back to be punished." He shook his head and stared at the floor in front of him. "How can children be robbed of their childhood?"

"I'm not trying to make excuses for the abusers, but I believe that's nothing new. Children have been abused and used as slaves throughout history. Children as young as five were forced up chimneys or set to work in the coal mines."

He inhaled a sharp breath. "You're right, of course. Mankind has taken advantage and made many mistakes throughout history, and it's usually the younger generation that has suffered. With respect, and I don't think it's a competition in who suffered more, but to be abused and tortured at the tender age of eight onwards is, well, inconceivable."

"I agree with you. I'm sorry we can't stay longer; we must get back to the station. I just wanted to touch base with you, to let you know that we're taking your correspondence very seriously indeed and that we have discovered several bodies at the site. Three from the lake itself. I know that information is safe with you."

"In a way, I'm heartbroken that some of my friends lost their lives, but I'm relieved that their remains have been found. Will they be laid to rest?"

"You have my word that will happen. Are you up to giving us a statement? If so, I'll have a word with the desk sergeant when we get back and ask him to arrange a mutually convenient time for that to take place."

"Yes, by all means. Before you go, what's going to happen to the people involved in the crimes?"

"Again, this is for your ears only. We're aware of three teachers who were still alive. We visited one in a care home; unfortunately, he died while we were on the premises. Another man in the care home is too far gone with dementia for us to interview. We also visited a third man, and he was supposed to turn up at the station to be interviewed today, but he killed himself and his wife at the same time."

"What the...? Bloody coward. But why kill his wife?"

"Because he was her full-time carer. I suppose he couldn't face spending the rest of his time in prison, leaving her to fend for herself."

"I don't know what to say about that. On the one hand, he's a selfish prick, but then, on the other, I guess people will say he had his wife's best interests at heart. When the news comes out about what he did to the pupils, the public is going to think it's all nonsense."

"Don't worry, you have my word that won't happen. Are you going to be okay?"

"I think so. The more I sit here thinking about things, the more I realise that I did the right thing by getting in touch with you. Again, thank you for listening to my ramblings and taking a chance."

Sally and Lorne rose from the sofa.

"No, it should be me thanking you," Sally said. "I can't imagine what you must have been through over the years."

"Let's not go there. The nightmares have been terrifying, to the point that I've forced myself to remain awake some nights."

He showed them to the front door.

Sally rubbed his upper arm. "Hopefully, you'll be able to sleep much better from this day forward. Take care of yourself."

"I hope so. Thanks to you and your wonderful team. How long will it take them to complete the search of Oakridge?"

"We don't know. It might be weeks or even months. It depends on what other work they need to attend to in between. It's like every other department, short of resources. However, the good news is that they've made an excellent start."

"Either way, you'll have me, and the other boys' families, behind you."

"We're still digging. Hopefully, before long, we'll find more perpetrators we can bring to justice." Sally leaned in and whispered, "With Carol's help, I'm sure that will not take long."

He tapped the side of his nose. "Your secret is safe with me. Although watching the news, some reporters have already let the cat out of the bag."

"Don't worry. It's the results we achieve that matter. It was nice meeting you. Try to be kind to yourself. Can you go away for a few days?"

"No, I'll stick around and see what happens. Don't forget, I need to give you my statement, as well."

"I'll sort that out as soon as we return to the station." Sally smiled and left the house.

Lorne was already standing by the car.

"What a lovely man," Lorne said.

"I'm glad he ran away and escaped the horrors that his friends had to endure; which ultimately ended their lives."

"He realises how lucky he was. Let's hope we can find at

least one person to punish. If only he'd come forward years ago."

"You're forgetting, he tried to, but his complaint was brushed aside. Truth be told, he logged his complaints with men and not female officers who were likely to take his complaints seriously."

"I'm so glad you pursued this case. All credit to you, Sally, you're one in a million."

"There's no I in team, Lorne. You should know that better than anyone."

"I do. We've done well, haven't we?"

"With Carol's help. Come on, let's get a wriggle on."

9

Two ladies were sitting in the reception area, waiting to see Sally when they arrived back at the station. Pat grabbed her attention before she could key in her number to the security door that led upstairs.

He lowered his voice and said, "They've come in to have a chat with you, ma'am. It's to do with your ongoing investigation."

Sally peered over her shoulder at the couple in their seventies or eighties and then faced Pat to ask, "Who are they?"

"Joy Bradley and Maria Cotton."

"I recognise the name Cotton, but Bradley isn't ringing a bell at all. Are they happy to speak with me together, or would they...? It doesn't matter, I'll ask them myself." She turned and approached the two women. "Hello, I'm DI Sally Parker. The desk sergeant informed me you would like to discuss the current investigation I'm handling."

The women's hands were linked.

"Yes, I'm Joy Bradley. My son, Daniel, went missing from Oakridge Hall."

"And I'm Maria Cotton. My son, Michael, also went missing from the hall. We saw on the news last night that a thorough search was taking place at the hall. Can you tell us why?"

"I'm pleased to meet you. Thank you for coming in to see me. Why don't we talk about this elsewhere?" Sally turned to Pat and Lorne. "Pat, is there an interview room available?"

"Room One, ma'am."

"Can you arrange for some drinks to be made for these ladies, please?"

"Thank you, a tea for me," Joy said.

"I prefer coffee, white, one sugar. Thank you," Maria added.

"And for you, ma'am?"

"Yes, Lorne and I will have our usual. Thanks, Pat. If you'd like to come this way, ladies. Please, there's no need for you to be worried about this experience."

"We're not. Well, maybe a little. All we want is to know the truth that has been hidden from us all these years," Maria said.

"I won't keep anything from you. I can promise you that."

Once they were settled in the interview room and their drinks had arrived, Sally asked, "Who wants to go first?" She smiled, trying to reassure the ladies that they were in safe hands and that they'd done the right thing coming forward.

The ladies glanced at each other.

Joy said, "I don't mind going first, if that's okay with you, Maria?"

"I think that's a good idea. I'm too nervous to speak right now."

"There's no need to be nervous," Sally said, her smile fixed in place.

Joy removed her hand from Maria's and wrung her hands together until the knuckles went white. "It's been so many years. We never forgot them. You have to believe that."

"We do. I promise we're not here to judge you, only to help ease your pain."

"Can you tell us if they've found anything at the school?"

"Why don't you tell me what you know first, and we'll go from there?"

"We've both been through hell over the years. My story is that Daniel was nine when he went missing. We received a call from the headmaster, Mr Gorman. He told us that Daniel had taken part in the yearly sport's day and then disappeared without a trace."

"Did they conduct a search for him?"

"Yes, the police got involved back then, too. It only lasted for a day. The officer in charge told us he'd spoken to several of the pupils, and they had reported that Daniel wasn't happy at home and was going to run away." She sniffed and shook her head. "That was news to me. Daniel was a sweet child, always giving me cuddles when we were alone. I thought it was a pack of lies they were telling me. I told the officer in charge as much, and he brushed my concerns aside as if they didn't matter." She fell silent, and her gaze dropped to the table. "His disappearance caused problems between my husband and I. I know I shouldn't have done it. There were no foundations for the accusation... I accused Sid of killing our son. I knew it wasn't in Daniel to just take off. The school was adamant he was happy there, so I thought accusing my husband was the only thing left for me to do."

"And what did your husband say?"

"He went ballistic. Was gutted that I could ever think him capable of hurting our son. But I had nothing else to cling to. Daniel was a carefree boy, and I couldn't think of a reason he would want to run away like that."

"Did your marriage last?" Sally asked.

"No. Sid drank himself to death a week later. He left me a note, telling me he had never laid a finger on our son, and that he could no longer live with the shame that I would believe he could harm him. Within a week, I had lost my son and my husband, and no one seemed to care. The police didn't want to know. The school appeared to wipe their hands of me because they said Daniel was no longer their responsibility if he'd run off. I didn't know where to turn to for help. We, sorry, I, didn't have the funds to employ a private investigator if there was such a thing back then. I've been living in limbo ever since, until today. They said on the news that you're working with a psychic. Is that true?"

"It is. Can I hear what Maria has to tell me, first? Then I'll explain where we are with the case."

"Yes, of course. Sorry, we both have ghastly tales to tell, that have blighted our lives for years. Go on, Maria, tell the inspector what you know."

Maria inhaled and exhaled a shuddering breath. "I'll try. I've locked it away for so many years…"

"I can understand and sympathise with you for doing that. Take your time. We're in no rush."

"It was around Christmastime, 1974. The first I heard something was wrong was when the headmaster rang me. Michael didn't board at the school; he was one of the lucky ones who came home every night. We'd heard the school was gaining an excellent reputation and were eager to get him there. Anyway, he stayed behind this particular night because they were holding a practice session for the choir. There was talk that the local mayor was lined up to attend the Christmas Choir event the school was putting on two days before Christmas. I was thrilled for him to be involved. He was chuffed they had asked him, too. Anyway, time was marching on, and it was already nine o'clock. I had paced the floor because Mickey, as we called him, told me he wouldn't be any later than eight-thirty. The school had arranged for the boys to be dropped off after practice."

"And he wasn't?"

"No. The headmaster rang me at around ten to tell me that Mickey had run off. He hadn't got on the bus because he'd argued with one of the other boys. He wasn't the type to do that, so I found that hard to believe. The headmaster swore it was the truth and refused to speak with me after that because he thought I was calling him a liar. I should have known then that something bad had happened to Mickey. For years, I clung to the belief that he was still out there somewhere and he'd return home soon. But that wasn't the case. Weeks turned into months and the months turned into years and, still, we received nothing. Mickey wasn't the type to just vanish into thin air. As a family, we were very close. My husband and I held a vigil for him every Friday night. It was the day of the week he went missing. We still light a candle for him today." She finished talking and reached for her friend's hand. "It's the not knowing what has happened to our sons over the years that drew us together."

"Both our sons were good boys. They wouldn't have had it in them to run away, despite what the headmaster told us. Please, if you know anything, will you tell us?" Joy pleaded.

Sally looked into the women's eyes and saw nothing but

sorrow and hurt. She felt sick to her stomach knowing that they had been crying out for news about their sons for years. Sally knew that Carol had mentioned Michael as being one of the children found in shackles in the secret room, but she couldn't recollect Daniel Bradley's name being mentioned before today. She was in a dilemma about what to do next until Lorne nudged her leg. "Okay, I wouldn't normally suggest this, but I think it might be a good idea if you both spoke to Carol. She's the psychic Sergeant Warner and I have been working with for years. How would you feel about that?" Sally glanced at Lorne, searching for her approval.

Lorne gave a brief nod.

Both women gasped and clung tighter to each other's hands.

"What do you think, Joy?" Maria asked.

Sally sensed the hesitation in both women and felt the need to add, "There's no pressure here, ladies. I know there are people out there who refuse to believe in the spirit world. Honestly, I used to be one of them until I met Carol. She's amazing and has already conversed with a few spirits when we visited the hall earlier today."

"What? Were any of them our sons?" Maria asked, her eyes widening.

"Possibly. I don't want to get your hopes up. All I'm trying to do is give you some form of closure after years of living with the unknown. What do you think? I'll tell you what, we'll leave you alone for a few minutes and let you have a chat about how you want to proceed."

"Thank you, we'd appreciate that, wouldn't we, Maria?" Joy said, colour rising in her cheeks.

Sally and Lorne left the room.

Outside, Sally rang the office and spoke to Stuart, "Hi,

it's me. We're downstairs and have just interviewed two ladies whose sons went missing at the school. I've given them the option to have a chat with Carol. I know I should have checked with her first before suggesting it. Can you do me a favour and run the idea past her?"

Stuart laughed. "Sorry, I don't mean to appear rude, boss. I think Carol must have heard you. She's nodding and already out of her seat on the way to the door."

"That's great news. I'll meet her at the bottom of the stairs. Hopefully, the two women will go ahead." Sally ended the call as the door opened.

Joy was standing there, shuffling her feet as she spoke. "We've agreed to give it a go on one proviso."

"Name it."

"That we can stop if it all becomes too overwhelming for us."

"Of course. Your rules, we're just happy to lend a hand. I'm sure you'll find the exercise very cathartic."

"I hope so."

"Take a seat. Would you like another drink?"

"Maybe some water this time, thank you."

"Lorne, can you sort that out for me while I ask Carol to join us?"

"Consider it done."

Joy returned to the room to sit with Maria. Sally and Lorne walked up the corridor together, punching the air because their plan had worked.

"I'll be two secs," Lorne said. She glanced up the stairs and smiled at Carol. "Are you sure you're up for this, love?"

"Lead the way. These ladies have a right to know what happened to their sons."

Sally cringed. "They're a bit apprehensive, so go easy on them, Carol."

"You do your job and leave me to do mine. I'd prefer to see them separately if the ladies are agreeable? I promise I won't reveal anything too graphic."

"I've got no qualms about that, Carol. Just watch out for any signs of stress with them."

"Don't worry, I will."

Sally entered the interview room with Carol and introduced her to Joy and Maria. "This is Carol, the lady with an extraordinary talent."

"Oh, you look so normal," Maria said, then slapped her hand over her mouth. Dropping it, she added, "I'm sorry that sounded rude. I didn't mean it that way."

Carol smiled. "Please, it's fine, don't worry. I'm pleased to meet you both. Who wants to go first?"

Joy tentatively raised her hand. "I will."

"Let's see if the room next door is free and you can use that," Sally said. She knocked on the door to Interview Room Two and opened it to find it was empty. "All clear," she called.

Carol stood back and allowed Joy to go ahead. "We won't be long."

"We'll be next door, keeping Maria company. Please don't worry, Joy, you're in safe hands."

"Thank you," Joy said as she sat down.

Half an hour later, after both women had spoken with Carol, Sally led them back to the reception area. Joy and Maria clung to each other, both tearful and overwhelmed but grateful for the experience.

"We can't thank you enough, Inspector," Maria said. "We are feeling a shared sense of relief and gratitude for the opportunity to connect with our sons today. Carol was wonderful. I will never doubt the abilities of a psychic ever again."

"She is one in a million. Be warned, though, there are dozens of charlatans out there."

"We won't need to see anyone else. She made a promise that, now Daniel and Michael have connected with us, they will proceed towards the completion of their journey. They'll also be the first to greet us when our time comes to leave this world."

Sally's eyes pricked with tears. She cleared her throat and gave each of them a hug. "I'm so pleased you could get closure. I want to assure you that we will do our very best to ensure that those who caused your sons' deaths are punished."

"Are they still alive?" Joy asked.

Sally tilted her hand from side to side. "We're still searching and won't give up hope until we've found someone alive. I realise that this may offer little solace to you, but given the significant time that has transpired since the crimes were committed, it is the best outcome we can strive for."

"We understand. If nothing further comes of this, at least we've interacted with our sons' spirits today. We'll always be grateful to you for that."

"Thank you. That means a lot. I'll be in touch with you soon if any news comes our way." Sally opened the main door and waved the two ladies off, then joined the rest of the team upstairs. "I'm knackered. I can only imagine how you're feeling, Carol. Thank you for speaking to Joy and Maria. You've made their day."

"More like their year," Lorne was quick to add.

"Yes, you're probably right. How were they?"

"Reluctant to go with the flow at first until I gave each of them a snippet of information which was private between each boy and his mum, then they became receptive and got a lot from the experience. They'll sleep better tonight, knowing that their boys' bodies have been found and can be laid to rest at last."

Sally smiled. "Okay, now all we have to do is find someone who is still alive that we can hold accountable for their deaths."

"Give me the ledgers. Or take me to them and leave me with them for a while," Carol said.

"They're with Stuart. There are quite a few to go through."

"Then I'd better get on with it, hadn't I?"

Stuart and Jordan moved from their seats to allow Carol access to the ledgers.

"Can you give me a clean sheet of paper?" She turned her head away to avoid seeing the notes the two men had already made. "I don't want to see what you've found. Let's go with the facts, shall we?"

Stuart removed his notebook, and he and Jordan relocated to the seats on the other side of the room. Carol was left alone for the next couple of hours to do her thing.

Sally kept a close eye on her and was the first to react when Carol sat back in her chair and looked at the ceiling. She darted across the room to check if everything was all right.

"Carol, are you okay?"

"Yes. I just need a few minutes to recharge my battery. It's a pity I no longer smoke." She smiled and handed Sally the notes she'd made. "Let me know if you need help to decipher what I've written. Some of it was scribbled in a hurry."

"I will." Sally stared down at the comprehensive notes, and her mouth gaped open. Once she'd recovered from the shock, she whispered, "Oh my, I recognise some of these names. Are you telling me they all visited the boys at the school?"

"Worse, those are the names of the individuals the boys told me killed one or more boys at the school."

Sally shook her head in disbelief and then hugged Carol. "You've saved us hours and hours of work."

Carol raised a finger as a warning. "You're still going to need to find the evidence the men were there, which you will do."

Sally frowned and inclined her head. "What do you mean?"

"There's a secret room on the first floor that the techs will uncover soon. Inside, you'll find the security equipment the headmaster used to film the dignitaries arriving. He was a crafty bugger, never trusted any of them."

Lorne gasped. "So, he filmed everyone arriving, in case they had a change of heart about paying the vast sums of money they handed over to be with the boys?"

"What? No, really?" Sally asked. "Shit, I'm eager to get back out there and punch a few holes in the walls myself," she added, finding her second wind from somewhere.

"Me, too. Maybe we can do that tomorrow. It's been a hell of a day. I think it's taken its toll on all of us," Carol said.

"I'm going to check in with the chief and then call it a day. You folks go ahead. I'll see you all in the morning."

"We'll have to wait for you," Lorne reminded her.

Sally cringed. "Sorry, of course. I won't be long. He's usually eager to sign off as much as we are."

After Lyn allowed Sally in to see DCI Green, she sat with him for fifteen minutes to bring him up to date regarding the investigation. He sat there in silence, astounded by what she had revealed, and studied the list.

"I know some of these people." He shook his head in disgust. "Most of them are dead now. More's the pity. But this man is still alive." He ran his finger under the name of Robert Hopwood. "He was one of the youngest superintendents of the day."

"Do you know where he is now?"

"Yes, he still lives in the area. I think he recently buried his wife. Shit, he's in his nineties now, Sally. Confronting him with the evidence will probably kill him."

She shrugged. "What are you suggesting? That the facts remain hidden and he gets away with it until the day he dies?"

"Don't say it like that. That's not what I meant, and you know it." He ran a hand through his greying hair. "Shit, sorry to put the cat amongst the pigeons, but this is above my pay grade, and yours come to that. I'm going to have to run it past the superintendent in the morning." His attention was drawn back to the list again. "Patrick Jackson, the mayor at the time is on the list, too. I think he's still around, albeit in his eighties now, but I believe they're still reliant on him down at the council for helping to organise fundraisers and such like."

"Shit! How are we going to handle it, sir? Not wishing to pass the buck here but, as you said, all of this is above our pay grade, saying that these men have killed innocent children. I'm not prepared to brush it under the carpet, and neither should you."

"I have no intention of doing that, I assure you. Let me talk with the superintendent in the morning and I'll get back to you right away. It's not something I'd want to bother him with at this time of the day."

Sally stared at him and shook her head. "I think you're wrong but, on the other hand, the victims have waited fifty years for justice. I don't suppose an extra few hours will matter."

"Exactly. Will you pass on my thanks to your psychic friend? She's done a wonderful job, pointing us in the right direction of the evidence. It's what we're going to need to bring these bastards to court."

"I will, sir. Goodnight." She left the room feeling a tad dejected but tried to dismiss it on her way back to the office. "Right, are you ready, ladies?" She did her best to sound upbeat and avoided eye contact with Carol.

"How did it go?" Carol asked.

"Okay. We're going to discuss it further in the morning, once he's gone over the facts this evening."

Carol shook her head. "There's no reason for you to lie to us, Sally."

She slumped against the wall beside her. "I'm sorry. He's going to run it past the superintendent in the morning. Robert Hopwood used to be a popular superintendent back in the day. As for the ex-mayor, Patrick Jackson, he's still in the limelight today and often organises charity events et cetera for the council. We, or should I say, the chief decided this was above our pay grade and we'd need extra backup before taking it further."

"Not the best news to hear, but I understand where your chief is coming from, Sally. Thank you for being honest with us."

"Always, Carol. We'll get the bastards, I promise you. Let's go home. I don't know about you two, but I'm famished."

"We were just saying the same. I rang Tony. He told me it's dinner at your place again tonight. I hope that's okay with you?" Lorne said.

"I'm delighted. It'll be good to have a chat over a glass of wine and a sumptuous dinner. Did he tell you what was on the menu?"

"Salmon."

"Sounds lovely. Shall I drop you back home first?"

"Yes, please. We could both do with a shower after being at the hall today."

"That makes three of us. While I think of it, would you both be up to coming back to the hall with me in the morning?"

"To find the secret room?" Carol asked.

"Yes. I think we're going to need to find the extra proof needed to bring these two down. They'll probably have all the excuses under the sun stored in their brains, ready to let loose if the truth ever surfaced. I'd like to hit them with the evidence and see them try to get out of that particular hole."

"I agree," Carol replied.

They all hugged and then set off for the evening.

EPILOGUE

At nine-thirty the following morning, they met up with Pauline and her team at Oakridge Hall.

"Hi, don't mind us. We'll keep out of your hair today. We'll be upstairs, having a snoop around," Sally said.

Pauline's gaze dropped to the lump hammer Lorne was holding. "With that?" She sighed. "I've got too much on my plate to argue with you. Do what you want, just keep out of our way."

"That's our intention. Have you discovered any other bodies?"

"Not yet."

"We spoke to two ladies yesterday, both of whom had lost sons who attended the school. Carol picked up that one boy's body was weighted down in the lake, and the other was the boy we found in shackles in the first room we discovered."

Pauline hitched up her eyebrows. "And how did that go?"

"Very well. The women were pleased that their bodies

had been found and they could go on to their final resting place."

"Glad to hear it. I must get on." Pauline dismissed them with a wave and ran up the steps to the hall.

"Ignore her," Carol said. "She's emotionally wrought right now, concerned with the personal stuff she needs to attend to."

"I hope it's nothing serious, for her sake," Sally said. "Maybe I should offer her a shoulder to cry on?"

Carol shook her head. "I would leave well alone. Let her come to you if she needs to."

They entered the house.

Carol paused and smiled in the entrance hall. "The spirits are quieter today as if they're pleased with how the investigation is going, if that makes sense?"

"It does."

They went upstairs and left Carol to wander the corridor, to see what vibes she could pick up.

Halfway down, Carol pointed to a room on her right. "I think we should try this one first. It's at the front, above the main door. It makes sense that it should be here."

Sally and Lorne joined her. They entered the room together and stood in the middle. Carol placed her hand on three of the internal walls. After going back to the first wall she had touched, she left the room to see what was next door. Sally watched her open a door in between the two rooms. It was a linen cupboard, packed with towels and tablecloths that were still in reasonable condition.

Carol brushed past Sally and announced. "It's here, behind the linen cupboard. The headmaster had a security room installed."

"Allow me." Lorne raised the hammer several times and punched a hole the size of a football in the plasterboard.

Sally was the first to peer into the opening. "You were spot on, as usual, Carol. Christ, do you want a job?"

They all laughed, but it soon died down as the seriousness of the situation dawned on them.

"We're going to have to do this ourselves," Sally said. "The SOCO team are up to their necks elsewhere."

Lorne raised the hammer. "It'll take a while to break through with this thing."

"I'll call Simon and see if he and Tony can lend us a hand." She removed her phone from her pocket and punched the number one on her phone. "Hey, it's me. Are you busy?"

"Not particularly. Why, what do you need?"

"The hammer you gave us did the trick of locating the secret room, but we could do with something else to help us finish the job."

"We've got just the thing. We'll see you shortly."

Simon and Tony arrived within fifteen minutes with a sledgehammer. Tony insisted he should do the work and asked the others to stand back and cover their mouths because of the dust. The three women thought it would be better for them to leave the room, instead. It proved to be the wisest move, as the dust cloud was unbelievable once Tony's efforts paid off.

With the wall demolished, they were all astonished to see the amount of equipment stored inside the room.

"Wow, he really meant business, didn't he? Devious sod," Sally muttered.

"Let's hope you find what you're looking for, ladies. We'll get back to our day jobs now, if you don't mind?" Simon kissed Sally on the cheek and left the room.

"My hero," Lorne said and kissed Tony on the lips, then wiped the dust from her mouth. "You might need to go home and have a shower before you get on with your day."

He nodded. "It's at the top of my list. I'll see you later. Thanks for allowing me to let off some steam today."

Sally arrived back at the station hours later and placed a box full of tapes on the chief's desk. "Here's the evidence you need to nail the bastards, sir."

"What? How did you find it?"

"I told you, there was a secret room that we wouldn't have known about if we hadn't had Carol working alongside us. They're tapes. We'll need to send them off to the lab. They'll have the equipment on hand to view them. We haven't."

"So, we're still none the wiser about what we have here?" He rifled through the box.

"I shouldn't need to present you with further evidence, but we went the extra mile and got it for you. It's up to you to do the right thing now, sir."

He sat again and sighed. "Leave me to make the call to the superintendent. I'll get back to you soon, I promise."

"Thank you, sir. Good luck. There's a lot at stake here."

"I'm aware of that, Inspector."

Sally left the room and walked back to the office with a sense of foreboding travelling with her.

"Well, how did you get on?" Lorne asked.

"He's contacting the superintendent now. We need to keep our fingers and toes crossed on this one."

"You're worrying unnecessarily. The superintendent is a stickler for doing the right thing. You're going to need to trust his decision, ladies," Carol said and sank into the chair beside her.

"You look wrung out. All this has been too much for you,

hasn't it?" Lorne asked. She placed a hand on her friend's shoulder.

"I'll be all right. I just need to have a rest for five minutes."

"Why don't you go in my office?" Sally suggested.

"No, I'm fine as I am. Stop fussing over me."

An hour later, DCI Green visited them. Sally introduced him to Carol. He seemed uncomfortable to have her there while he shared the news.

"You can trust her, sir. You won't reveal anything that has been said in this office, will you, Carol?"

"I never have in the past, have I, Lorne?"

"Never. I'd trust Carol with my life, and I have in the past."

"Okay, okay, there's no need to say anything further. I had to come here in person to share the good news with you all. The superintendent wanted me to pass on his congratulations for the effort you've put into this investigation. The evidence you have presented will prove to be the downfall of those involved in these heinous crimes. He's going to personally speak with the CPS and make sure those who are still alive are punished for the crimes they committed."

Sally and Lorne high-fived each other.

"That's the best news we could have hoped to receive today, sir. Thank you," Sally replied. A calmness descended like she'd never known before after wrapping up a case. "I might add, all this is down to Carol. Without her help, none of this would have been possible."

The chief took a step towards Carol. "We'll be forever grateful for your input. You have an amazing talent, dear lady."

Carol blushed as he shook her hand. "Thank you. The

tortured souls guided me, longing for the truth to be heard. They're surrounding me now, applauding you all."

The hairs on the back of Sally's neck rose, but she resisted the temptation to shudder.

The chief freaked out and backed up to the door. "On that note, I'll bid you farewell. Congratulations to everyone."

Carol covered her mouth until he left the room and then laughed. "I thought that would freak him out."

The room erupted, and Stuart stood to make everyone a coffee. He handed them around and said, "This deserves a toast. To Carol, Psychic Extraordinaire. I was a sceptic until I saw you in action. It's been a pleasure working with you."

"Thank you, Stuart, for your kind words, although I believe everyone deserves praise for the effort they have all put in."

They all patted each other on the back for the next five minutes. The only regret Sally had was that they hadn't identified the mystery caller, who had warned them off.

Sally nudged Lorne and whispered, "Is Carol all right? Why don't you borrow my car and take her home so that she can rest?"

"I'll ask."

They both approached Carol.

"Sally suggested I take you back to our place so you can rest properly," Lorne said.

Carol glanced up at her and shook her head. "No, I have to go home... and you need to come with me, Lorne."

"What are you talking about? I can't. I have a job to do here." Lorne faced Sally and shrugged.

"What are you trying to tell her, Carol?" Sally asked.

"We have to go now... Charlie's life is in danger."

THE END

THANK you for reading Echoes of Silence, the next thrilling adventure is The Final Betrayal

HAVE you read any of my other fast-paced crime thrillers yet?
Why not try the first book in the DI Sara Ramsey series
No Right To Kill

OR GRAB the first book in the bestselling, award-winning, Justice series here, Cruel Justice

OR THE FIRST book in the spin-off Justice Again series,
Gone in Seconds

MAYBE YOU'D PREFER my thriller series set in the stunning Lake District, the first book is To Die For

PERHAPS YOU'D PREFER to try one of my other police procedural series, the DI Kayli Bright series which begins with
The Missing Children

OR MAYBE YOU'D enjoy the DI Sally Parker series set in Norfolk,
Wrong Place

. . .

OR MY GRITTY police procedural starring DI Nelson set in Manchester, Torn Apart

OR MAYBE YOU'D like to try one of my successful psychological thrillers I know The Truth or She's Gone or Shattered Lives

KEEP IN TOUCH WITH M A COMLEY

Newsletter
http://smarturl.it/8jtcvv

BookBub
www.bookbub.com/authors/m-a-comley

Blog
http://melcomley.blogspot.com

Facebook Readers' Page
https://www.facebook.com/groups/2498593423507951

TikTok
https://www.tiktok.com/@melcomley

ALSO BY M A COMLEY

Blind Justice (Novella)

Cruel Justice (Book #1)

Mortal Justice (Novella)

Impeding Justice (Book #2)

Final Justice (Book #3)

Foul Justice (Book #4)

Guaranteed Justice (Book #5)

Ultimate Justice (Book #6)

Virtual Justice (Book #7)

Hostile Justice (Book #8)

Tortured Justice (Book #9)

Rough Justice (Book #10)

Dubious Justice (Book #11)

Calculated Justice (Book #12)

Twisted Justice (Book #13)

Justice at Christmas (Short Story)

Prime Justice (Book #14)

Heroic Justice (Book #15)

Shameful Justice (Book #16)

Immoral Justice (Book #17)

Toxic Justice (Book #18)

Overdue Justice (Book #19)

Unfair Justice (a 10,000 word short story)

Irrational Justice (a 10,000 word short story)

Seeking Justice (a 15,000 word novella)

Caring For Justice (a 24,000 word novella)

Savage Justice (a 17,000 word novella)

Justice at Christmas #2 (a 15,000 word novella)

Gone in Seconds (Justice Again series #1)

Ultimate Dilemma (Justice Again series #2)

Shot of Silence (Justice Again series #3)

Taste of Fury (Justice Again series #4)

Crying Shame (Justice Again series #5)

To Die For (DI Sam Cobbs #1)

To Silence Them (DI Sam Cobbs #2)

To Make Them Pay (DI Sam Cobbs #3)

To Prove Fatal (DI Sam Cobbs #4)

To Condemn Them (DI Sam Cobbs #5)

To Punish Them (DI Sam Cobbs #6)

To Entice Them (DI Sam Cobbs #7)

To Control Them (DI Sam Cobbs #8)

To Endanger Lives (DI Sam Cobbs #9)

To Hold Responsible (DI Sam Cobbs #10)

To Catch a Killer (DI Sam Cobbs #11)

To Believe the Truth (DI Sam Cobbs #12)

To Blame Them (DI Sam Cobbs 13)

To Judge Them (DI Sam Cobbs #14)

To Fear Him (DI Sam Cobbs #15)

To Deceive Them (DI Sam Cobbs #16)

Forever Watching You (DI Miranda Carr thriller)

Wrong Place (DI Sally Parker thriller #1)
No Hiding Place (DI Sally Parker thriller #2)
Cold Case (DI Sally Parker thriller #3)
Deadly Encounter (DI Sally Parker thriller #4)
Lost Innocence (DI Sally Parker thriller #5)
Goodbye My Precious Child (DI Sally Parker #6)
The Missing Wife (DI Sally Parker #7)
Truth or Dare (DI Sally Parker #8)
Where Did She Go? (DI Sally Parker #9)
Sinner (DI Sally Parker #10)
The Good Die Young (DI Sally Parker #11)
Coping Without You (DI Sally Parker #12)
Could It Be Him (DI Sally Parker #13)
Frozen In Time (DI Sally Parker #14)
Echoes of Silence (DI Sally Parker #15)
The Final Betrayal (DI Sally Parker #16)
Web of Deceit (DI Sally Parker Novella)

The Missing Children (DI Kayli Bright #1)
Killer On The Run (DI Kayli Bright #2)
Hidden Agenda (DI Kayli Bright #3)
Murderous Betrayal (Kayli Bright #4)
Dying Breath (Kayli Bright #5)
Taken (DI Kayli Bright #6)
The Hostage Takers (DI Kayli Bright Novella)

No Right to Kill (DI Sara Ramsey #1)

Killer Blow (DI Sara Ramsey #2)

The Dead Can't Speak (DI Sara Ramsey #3)

Deluded (DI Sara Ramsey #4)

The Murder Pact (DI Sara Ramsey #5)

Twisted Revenge (DI Sara Ramsey #6)

The Lies She Told (DI Sara Ramsey #7)

For The Love Of... (DI Sara Ramsey #8)

Run for Your Life (DI Sara Ramsey #9)

Cold Mercy (DI Sara Ramsey #10)

Sign of Evil (DI Sara Ramsey #11)

Indefensible (DI Sara Ramsey #12)

Locked Away (DI Sara Ramsey #13)

I Can See You (DI Sara Ramsey #14)

The Kill List (DI Sara Ramsey #15)

Crossing The Line (DI Sara Ramsey #16)

Time to Kill (DI Sara Ramsey #17)

Deadly Passion (DI Sara Ramsey #18)

Son of the Dead (DI Sara Ramsey #19)

Evil Intent (DI Sara Ramsey #20)

The Games People Play (DI Sara Ramsey #21)

Revenge Streak (DI Sara Ramsey #22)

Seeking Retribution (DI Sara Ramsey #23)

Gone... But Where? (DI Sara Ramsey #24)

Last Man Standing (DI Sara Ramsey #25)

Vanished (DI Sara Ramsey #26)

I Know The Truth (A Psychological thriller)

She's Gone (A psychological thriller)

Shattered Lives (A psychological thriller)

Evil In Disguise – a novel based on True events

Deadly Act (Hero series novella)

Torn Apart (Hero series #1)

End Result (Hero series #2)

In Plain Sight (Hero Series #3)

Double Jeopardy (Hero Series #4)

Criminal Actions (Hero Series #5)

Regrets Mean Nothing (Hero series #6)

Prowlers (Di Hero Series #7)

Sole Intention (Intention series #1)

Grave Intention (Intention series #2)

Devious Intention (Intention #3)

Cozy mysteries

Murder at the Wedding

Murder at the Hotel

Murder by the Sea

Death on the Coast

Death By Association

Merry Widow (A Lorne Simpkins short story)

It's A Dog's Life (A Lorne Simpkins short story)

A Time To Heal (A Sweet Romance)

A Time For Change (A Sweet Romance)

High Spirits

The Temptation series (Romantic Suspense/New Adult Novellas)

Past Temptation

Lost Temptation

Clever Deception (co-written by Linda S Prather)

Tragic Deception (co-written by Linda S Prather)

Sinful Deception (co-written by Linda S Prather)

Printed in Dunstable, United Kingdom